White Wolf Mate

(SILVERLAKE SHIFTERS BOOK 2)

Anastasia Wilde

ISBN: 1539641694
ISBN-13: 978-1539641698

Published in the United States of America.

Books by This Author

Silverlake Shifters
Fugitive Mate
White Wolf Mate
Tiger Mate

Silverlake Enforcers
The Enforcers: KANE
The Enforcers: ISRAEL
The Enforcers: NOAH

Bad Blood Shifters
Bad Blood Bear
Bad Blood Wolf
Bad Blood Leopard
Bad Blood Panther
Bad Blood Alpha

Wild Dragons
Dragon's Rogue
Dragon's Rebel
Dragon's Storm

CONTENTS

CHAPTER 1

They were going to catch up with him soon.

Rafe Connors drove his motorcycle up the dark mountain road, towering pine trees blocking out the night sky. The road wound through the forest in steep curves, repeatedly sending his back wheel within inches of the rocky ravine on his right-hand side. Rain was falling in a light drizzle, and the sharp smell of mud and decayed leaves spun up from under his tires as he rode the edge.

He gunned the motor and the bike roared. He was driving too fast—he knew it. He was always driving too fast lately, going too far, in some kind of reckless compulsion.

Like tonight. There was no reason to pick a fight with those guys in that bar. They were humans, not shifters, just a bunch of ignorant rednecks spouting bullshit. He'd taken offense because he wanted to, goading them until one of them took a swing at him.

Then he'd kicked their asses.

He didn't have to. He could have walked away. But he couldn't help himself. He'd always had this restlessness, the inability to settle, the need to stir things up. Ever since their wolf pack had been scattered when he was just a kid.

But now it was getting worse.

It should have been getting better. The pack was coming back together. Jace, their alpha, had found his fated mate and bonded to her, sealing the pack's claim on Silverlake Mountain. They were getting organized. Everybody had a job, a purpose. The pack was growing bigger, settling into a family instead of a bunch of yahoo bikers taking odd jobs.

Yahoo bikers. Him and Jace and their best friend Jesse. And later, Kane and Israel. Even though Kane was an asshole and Israel barely talked to anybody but Kane, Rafe missed the bad old days, when it was just the five of them against the world.

He took a tight curve and the back wheel almost slid out from under him. He swerved to get the bike back under control. He'd better slow down…

And then he heard them coming up behind him. The roar of a pickup truck, the sharp echo of someone shooting at the moon. Whoops and hollers and rebel yells.

They were drunk as skunks, and they were pissed off. At him. And now they didn't have just fists and boots. They had trucks and guns—and he was totally unprotected on his bike. Shit.

He could ditch the bike and shift, but they still had the guns. And they'd destroy his bike, or steal it. No way he'd let that happen. Rafe loved his bike.

And face it, he loved a challenge. He couldn't outrun

them all the way to Silverlake, but he might make it to old Grizzly's cabin on Hawkeye Mountain. And if he didn't, well, he might as well go out in a blaze of glory, riding hard. At least, that's what he liked to tell himself. Who wanted to turn into an old fart, anyway?

Die young, stay pretty.

The road leveled out on a straightaway, and the truck headlights caught him in their glare. A bullet whined overhead, and the headlights grew brighter as the truck accelerated. Damn, somebody had a souped-up engine in their truck. They were driving like bigger idiots than he was, and closing fast.

He swerved again. The road was getting slicker, the rain coming down harder. That was going to be more of a problem for him than for them, unfortunately. He cut the headlight on his bike. He could see fine in the dark with his wolf vision, and it would make it harder for them to shoot him in the back.

They were taunting him now, yelling drunken insults. He risked a glance over his shoulder. The front truck had two in the cab, and at least two or three in the bed. And more in the second truck. They probably weren't shooting to kill. They'd be trying to wing him. Run him off the road. Destroy his bike. Beat the crap out of him.

As if.

There was another curve coming up—a sharp one that would slow them down. If he could give himself a big enough head start, he could make the turnoff to Grizzly's before they got him in sight. Send those assholes driving straight up the mountain before they realized he'd gotten away.

Adrenalin shot through his veins. He felt alive in a way he never felt in his normal everyday life. It was why he rode the edge, why he made the trouble.

He wasn't much good at anything else. Rafe Connors, always second. But he was good at this.

He swung around the curve in a controlled skid, one booted foot skimming the ground, letting the bike fishtail just enough to control the momentum. At the last second he gunned it toward the turnoff, spinning out and laying a patch on the slick asphalt.

Just as he punched it, she landed in the road in front of him. A white wolf, ghostly in the darkness, leaping down off the wooded slope.

Rafe barely missed her, swerving to his right. He couldn't control his speed, and his bike went shooting off over the edge of the road. Right down into the ravine.

He flung himself away from the bike so he wouldn't land underneath it, and he heard it crash just before his own body hit the rocks. He and the bike both rolled down the steep, rocky slope. Rafe felt excruciating pain as his leg bones snapped. The impact swung him around and he smashed his head on an outcropping. Even as he fell, he knew it was bad. Really bad. He rolled to the bottom of the ravine, which was full of scrub and bushes. He landed hard and something sharp impaled him through the shoulder, and he screamed. Then, mercifully, he came to a stop.

Every inch of him was on fire with pain. Above, he heard the trucks screech to a halt, and the sounds of doors opening and boots on the pavement. They were shouting to each other: "Holy shit!" "He went right over the edge." "There's his bike…" "Where the fuck is he?" "Fuckin' dead, man."

No, he just wished he was.

A flashlight shone down, its beam sweeping through the darkness.

"There he is!"

There was a silence. "*Day*um, he's fucked up," somebody said. "Think he's really dead?"

"Whether he is or not, we're screwed if anybody knows we were here," somebody else said. "We need to get out of here."

"Nah, man, we gotta see if he's still alive."

There was the sound of somebody starting to climb down the ravine.

"Don't do that, man. There's an easier way." He heard the sound of a round being pumped into a rifle chamber. Rafe groaned and tried to move, but he couldn't. Were they really going to shoot him while he was helpless at the bottom of a ravine? This was no friendly bar brawl. He'd definitely picked a fight with the wrong guys, and now he was going to go out—not in a blaze of glory, jumping his bike over the ravine or some other crazy stunt. But broken and bleeding, on the ground in the rain.

It figured. He couldn't even kill himself right.

He waited, eyes closed, for the sound of the shot.

Instead, he felt a rush of air as something big passed overhead.

The arguing voices overhead turned panicked. "Holy shit!"

"It's the ghost wolf! The fucker's dead, man!"

"Nah, it means somebody's about to die…"

"Shoot it!"

"You can't, asshole! It's a ghost!"

Rafe, through his haze of pain, heard the wolf snarl. She leaped from rock to rock, flowing gracefully up the ravine toward the group of men.

They panicked and scattered, heading for the trucks, leaving Rafe on the ground below. He didn't know whether to laugh or cry. Fuck. He'd really screwed himself this time. Jace would have to find somebody else to take over as the pack's second-in-command. Somebody better.

The last thing he heard before he passed out was the trucks skidding out, driving away as fast as they could.

And his last thought was, *Sorry, Jace.*

CHAPTER 2

Terin waited at the side of the road until she was certain the men had driven away. She wanted to make sure they didn't double back to hurt the man with the motorcycle.

She felt terrible about the accident. If she'd realized he was going to change direction like that, trying to make the turnoff at the last minute, she wouldn't have jumped into the road. She hadn't even realized people were chasing him. If she had, she would have done more to help. She knew how it felt to be hunted.

Finally, the sound of the engines faded and the night was quiet again. She turned and picked her way back down the ravine, still in her wolf form. It was raining harder now, the rocks wet beneath the pads of her paws.

The man lay in the brush at the bottom of the ravine, unconscious now. She could see he was breathing, but just barely. He looked a little older than she was— maybe late twenties. The rain and blood plastered his dark hair to his head. He looked strong and tough, but his mouth had a curl to it that suggested humor. And trouble.

She knew all about that.

She nosed at his face, but he didn't wake up. To her

surprise, he smelled like wolf. He must be a shifter, like her. She knew there were other shifters around here—a bear or two, some wildcats, and even a lynx far up the mountain. This one was probably from the wolf pack who had moved in over on Silverlake Mountain, a few years back. She'd made sure she never met any of them. She kept to herself—a lone wolf. The thought of a pack—of people around her all the time—made her feel like she couldn't breathe.

But she couldn't just leave him. He was really hurt bad. Leg broken in multiple places, and he'd hit his head. And a sharp branch was rammed straight through his upper chest, just under the shoulder. She couldn't tell if it had hit anything vital, but it had definitely broken his collarbone.

Even with shifter healing, she didn't think he'd last the night on his own. There was too much damage. And they were far from his pack—far from anywhere. No place to get help.

The only nearby shelter she knew of was a cave. She might be able to get him there; he was much bigger than she was, in human form, but she still had shifter strength. It would be rough going, in the rain, but it was probably his only chance.

She looked dubiously at his motorcycle. That was done for—it would have to stay. She'd take his saddlebags, though, in case there was anything useful inside.

She shifted to human form and grabbed the saddlebags. There was a strap that would let her hang them across her shoulders. She shivered a little. The rain was cold, and she didn't have any clothes. They were stashed in the cave with the rest of her supplies. Now that she had hands, she could check his injuries further. The leg was a mess—right now all she could do was splint it. She tore some pieces off his shirt and found some long, straight branches for splints. Luckily he had a knife in his bag, enabling her to cut the splints to size. There wasn't anything she could do about the head injury right now. She used the knife to cut the ends off the branch through his shoulder so it wouldn't bang into things while she carried him. Pulling it out now would just make him bleed more.

After she'd done all she could do, she squatted beside him. He looked so vulnerable lying there. She stroked his hair back from his forehead, and his eyes fluttered.

She breathed a sigh of relief. He wasn't gone yet. She hoped he was as strong as he looked. He was going to need strength. And so was she.

She heaved him up over her shoulders in a fireman's carry, her bare feet sliding a little as she staggered to get her balance. He weighed a ton.

Then she started up the slope on the far side of the ravine.

It was hard going. She had to use one arm to help her claw her way up the ravine, grabbing onto rocks and brush—anything that offered a handhold. That left only one arm to hang onto him, and try to keep him balanced over her shoulders. The rocks were getting slicker all the time, and twice she almost overbalanced and fell backwards. Her leg muscles burned like fire from the exertion, and her breath came in great gasps.

But finally, they were at the top. She took a brief rest, panting. Her hair was plastered to her face, and she shoved it away. She hoped this guy was worth it, and not just another yahoo like the guys who were chasing him.

She heaved him up on her shoulders again, and he gave a low moan. She couldn't imagine how much it must hurt him to be moved, but there was nothing she could do about that except hope he passed out again. Luckily, the cave wasn't far. Less than half a mile. A five-minute stroll in good weather, without carrying the dead weight of a man.

It took Terin much longer than that, but she finally got there. It was a good thing she was used to going barefoot through the woods, or her feet would have been a mess. As it was, she was bruised and battered.

But he was definitely in worse shape than she was.

She staggered through the mouth of the cave and laid him on the floor as gently as she could. At least it was dry inside, but it was pretty cold. Shifters didn't usually go into shock, but with the extent of his injuries, he might. She had to get him warm.

Luckily, she kept a stack of dry wood in here. The cave was one of her supply caches—she roamed all over the mountain as a wolf, far from her cabin, and it was always handy to have a place where she could shift safely and find clothes and food if she needed them.

And a warm fire.

She built one as quickly as she could, and then spread out a blanket and laid him gently onto it. She put some water on the fire to heat, and began cutting his clothes off. There wasn't much left of his shirt after she'd torn it up for bandages in the ravine, so that took no time. She needed his hunting knife for the jeans. It seemed as though the broken leg was the only serious injury on his legs, but the jeans still had to go. She'd never get him warm with all that wet cotton sapping his body heat.

He wasn't wearing any underwear. Even though he was unconscious, the unexpected sight of his muscular thighs and large cock sent a blush up her face and neck. *Focus,* she told herself. *He's hurt. How can you think about his cock at a time like this?*

She quickly covered his lower body with a blanket. First priority was the head wound. The shoulder wound was still bleeding, and could be more dangerous after she took the stick out, depending on what blood vessels had been hit. But if there was bleeding on his brain, he might not survive.

She cleaned the head wound as best she could. She couldn't feel any depression in the bones underneath it, like a skull fracture, and his pupils looked okay when she checked them. She'd just have to hope that his shifter healing abilities would handle whatever internal damage there was.

Then she moved to his leg. This was really bad. It looked like both bones in his lower leg were broken, and the knee was twisted. She bit her lip. She had to get that straightened out so that his shifter healing could do its work.

She had set broken bones once or twice before. At least none of these were sticking out through the skin. She felt his leg to see where the breaks were, and then braced herself to pull them straight.

Ten minutes later, she was sweaty and shaking, but the leg bones were realigned, and the kneecap was back in position. She'd done the best she could do. He'd woken up and screamed when she pulled the leg straight, but he'd passed out again right away. It was probably just as well.

She bound the splints back on, combed her drying hair back out of her face, and moved on to the chest wound.

Using the fairly clean back of his former shirt as a washrag, she dipped it in the warm water she'd heated, and began cleaning around the wound. His chest was broad and muscular, his abs chiseled like the ones on the cover models of the books she bought in the drugstore in town. She smoothed the damp cloth over them, entranced.

Her husband, Ben, had been short and wiry, and his abs had never looked like this. She'd never thought *any* guys actually looked like this—she'd figured the books exaggerated and the pictures on the covers were enhanced.

Apparently not.

She checked his breathing and his pulse again.

They'd improved, which was good. She just hoped she didn't undo all that when she pulled this stick out of him. If he'd damaged an artery and the stick was the only thing plugging the hole, he could bleed out in minutes—too fast for his shifter abilities to compensate.

But she couldn't leave it in there, either.

Taking a deep breath, she turned him on his side. Then she braced herself once more for leverage, grabbed the end of the stick, and pulled.

He arched his back, screaming. Seeing him in such pain made her feel like she was being stabbed in the heart, but she forced herself to ignore it. She pressed clean bandages to both sides of the wound, front and back.

Then she watched the white squares darken with blood, and waited, and prayed.

She didn't know why she needed so much to help this man. To save him. But she did.

The red stains grew larger, but not at an alarming rate. Terin kept pressure on both wounds.

After a few minutes, the bleeding slowed. Terin kept the pressure on a little longer, until it was nothing but a trickle. Then she sat back with a sigh of relief. His shifter healing was kicking in. He just might make it through the night.

She made up some new bandages and taped them to his chest with the surgical tape she kept in her first aid kit in the cave. Then she put more water on the fire to heat, taking some herbs from a pack that she kept in her supplies. He needed to drink something, since he'd lost

13

so much blood, and the herbs would help.

Now that he was stable, shock shouldn't be a problem. Not for a shifter. But she'd have to keep an eye on him until he regained consciousness. If he didn't wake up soon, she didn't know what she'd do.

She didn't want to get involved with people. She especially didn't want to get involved with a man. One had been enough. Now she had her place up the mountain, her cabin. She had her books and her paintings. Things were peaceful. No one bothered her.

The last thing she needed in her life was a man with sexy abs who rode motorcycles too fast.

CHAPTER 3

Rafe felt himself drifting in and out of consciousness. There was wet, and cold, and pain. And then hideous excruciating jolting, and more pain. And blackness.

And then there was a healing angel. Someone with soft hands, who touched him gently. After that, wrenching, screaming agony, followed by sweet relief. He didn't know where he was, except that it was warm. And there was a face, hovering above him.

A beautiful pale oval, with the bluest eyes he'd ever seen. So beautiful it must be a dream. Her hair was long and straight, and pale, pale blond—almost white. It shimmered in the firelight, dropping like a curtain when she dipped her head.

And she was naked. He could see her breasts—firm and lightly bronzed, as if she walked naked in the sun all the time. Or maybe lounged on a cloud. That thought made him smile. He was mesmerized; he'd never dreamed anyone so beautiful before. He reached out and cupped a breast, smoothing it with his hand, feeling the warmth and weight of it, the silkiness of her skin.

"Angel," he murmured.

Her eyes locked onto his, wide and shocked. For a

moment she went very still, like a hunted rabbit. And then she gently took his hand and laid it down by his side.

She pressed something down onto his chest, and pain shot through him. Shit. This was no dream. It was real. He felt like he'd been beaten up—or fallen down a ravine on his bike. Oh, right. He'd just done both. And now he'd grabbed the breast of a woman who was trying to help him.

Way to go, Rafe. Being your usual fuck-up self.

"Sorry," he slurred. "Dreaming. Thought you were…angel…"

A faint smile appeared on her face. She shook her head.

She turned away for a minute, and the firelight illuminated her hair like a halo. *Maybe she was an angel…*

She turned back, holding a steaming mug. It smelled evil. Rafe frowned.

"No…"

He tried to push it away, but she gently intercepted his hand. She supported him so he could sit up. Pain shot through his chest. And his head. And his leg. He winced. He drank a few swallows of the foul-tasting stuff and tried to lie back down, but she managed to be insistent without saying anything, coaxing him to drink the whole thing.

He did feel better afterwards. But he might have changed his mind about her being an angel.

She let him relax back, tucking something under his head for a pillow. "Thanks," he murmured, drifting.

There was no response, and he forced his eyes open again. He must have passed out for a minute, or an hour. She was kneeling by him again, this time wearing an oversized shirt.

"You...talk?" he slurred. If she'd said anything so far, he hadn't heard it.

She gave her head a slight shake, and then shrugged. His mind wouldn't put things together. A mute?

"S'okay," he said. "I talk enough for both've...us. Ever'body...always telling me...shut up."

That got another faint smile.

"Least...you have...sense of humor," he murmured.

She put her finger gently on his lips. Then she moved her hand over his eyes, to shut them. With great effort, he lifted his hand and took hers, kissing the palm, then the wrist.

"Thank you," he said. "And...sorry. 'Bout the breast thing. Touching...'thout permission...bad." He could feel himself drifting off, remembering the feel of her skin. "Was nice, though...."

CHAPTER 4

Terin watched him for a long time after he fell asleep. His breathing was steady and his temperature seemed normal, so there was probably no infection. Thank goodness for shifter immune systems. Now that she'd stopped the bleeding and set the bones, he should heal okay. The head injury didn't seem serious; he'd been awake and talking. She smiled to herself. He'd almost been making sense.

She studied him in the light of the fire. Dark brown hair turning into wild, unruly curls now that it was drying. She knew his eyes were dark too, though they'd shaded to golden when he was in pain. He'd nearly shifted while she was trying to set his leg, which would have been a disaster.

Strong jaw, vulnerable mouth, with that hint of humor in the way the corners turned up, even when he was asleep. She had a feeling he was a handful—wild, rebellious, restless. She could feel it in him; she'd seen it in the way he rode his motorcycle so recklessly.

There was an untamed spirit in him that spoke to hers. And he was…broken…inside. Like her. She hid her brokenness by retreating from the world, by being quiet.

Listening to the silence. That's the way she'd learned. She had a feeling he was different. That he tried escape his brokenness by running so fast it couldn't catch up to him. Riding fast. Riding the edges. Trying to keep ahead of it so it wouldn't drag him down.

They were so different.

And yet she found herself wanting to soothe him, calm that restless spirit and give it a place to rest. Fill the void with—something.

She touched her breast lightly through the shirt she wore. She could still feel the imprint of his hand, the way he'd cupped it, touched her reverently as if she were something impossibly beautiful and precious. An angel.

Sadness flooded through her. If he only knew. She was a demon, just like Ben had said. A monster. She'd panicked, and Ben had died. It was like she'd killed him—the only man who had been kind to her. And now she was alone, the way she was supposed to be. A lone wolf, just her and her paintings and her garden.

Ben. She didn't think about him as much anymore, not like it had been right after he died. After he'd turned on her. Gradually she'd erased his presence from the cabin. It was hers now, for better or worse. But she thought back now to how it had been with them.

She had slept with Ben, of course. Made love. It had been pleasant, comforting. He needed it more than she did, but it was something she could give him to repay him for everything he'd given her. And she'd liked it when he held her afterwards.

But she'd never felt the rush of feelings that this stranger evoked with a simple touch. The heat that had rushed through her, making her body tingle. The desire to touch him, to run her hands over the flat planes of his chest, to feel his arms around her, his body against hers, his hard cock inside her.

And the urge to protect him, to soothe him, to make him whole again.

It shook her world.

She lived alone; she had been alone too long to tolerate other people. She knew she wasn't like other people, or other wolves. She had been abandoned by her pack, her family. She couldn't even remember them—everything before Ben was a blank. She was broken and damaged, and the one person who'd cared for her didn't even want her once he knew what she was.

But there was still beauty in the world. When she was in her wolf form, she could see how beautiful the world was. She tried to put it into her paintings—the feel of the sun and the wind, the way the moon called to her at night, the vast deep mystery of the stars.

She wondered what this man would look like as a wolf. If he would see any beauty in her when she was changed into her true form. Or if he only could love the woman who looked like an angel.

She'd never know. She couldn't stay with him. She couldn't even let him know where she lived. His pack would want her territory, and then she'd be surrounded. Suffocated.

She gently stroked his hair back from his forehead.

She'd stay a little longer. Just until she was sure he was going to be okay. Then she'd go back to her real life, and he'd go back to his pack.

And they'd never see each other again.

CHAPTER 5

Rafe woke up with a beam of sunlight in his face. It took a second for him to realize where he was. The cave. He'd crashed his bike and been injured, and he'd ended up with some woman dragging him to a cave and tending his wounds.

An angel.

Most of what had happened to him after the crash was a blur of pain and confusion, but the memory of her was sharp and clear. Those stunning blue eyes, and the silky curtain of platinum hair, shining like a halo in the firelight.

She'd kept him alive.

He tentatively stretched his limbs. He was a little stiff, and definitely weak. And thirsty, but not as hungry and thirsty as he should have been. He vaguely remembered her pouring different drinks down his throat. Nasty-tasting, most of them, but it seemed like they'd done the trick.

He gingerly touched the place on his chest where he'd been impaled. *That* was something he'd pay money never to experience again. It was almost healed now, though. His leg was sore and his knee still hurt when he bent it, but he could feel that it was healing okay too.

And the damage to his head was mostly gone—he had a vague headache that was probably more hunger than anything else.

He wondered if she was coming back—his angel. Her scent had faded—it seemed like it had been at least twelve hours, maybe more, since she'd been here. He touched the fire pit. The ashes were mostly cold; only the embers buried deep inside were faintly warm.

How long had he been out? How long had he been here? He'd completely lost track of time, but to judge by how healed he was, he'd been in this cave for at least two days.

Shit. Nobody in the pack would have any idea what happened to him. Last they'd heard, he was going out for beers. They were used to him disappearing, though. Probably no one was even worried about him.

He wondered where his clothes were. They had to be a mess, but if he could patch something together he might have the option of hitching a ride home in human form, instead of going wolf and walking all the way.

He got up slowly, holding on to the wall while a head rush came and went. He put his weight on his bad leg and found out it would hold, though it was not happy. Then he explored the cave.

He was intrigued to find a stockpile of supplies. First aid, dried food, water, more nasty herbs. He snarfed down all the food and drank the water thirstily. He'd have to remember to come back and replace it. The woman obviously used this cave as some kind of supply dump, and the least he could do was repay what she'd used on him. There were also clothes in a plastic box—oversized men's shirts and jeans that looked like they'd fit her. Another, larger box was empty. Probably for the blankets he'd been lying on.

On top of that box was a clean set of clothes—men's work clothes. They might be a little tight, but they'd fit him. Next to that was the saddlebag from his bike, with all of his things intact and his motorcycle jacket inside. His gun was underneath it, with his extra ammo. Even his bandanna. And the things that had been in his pockets—wallet, change, knife, phone—were piled neatly next to it.

He picked up the phone and pushed the button. Dead. That figured. The charge had run out while he was unconscious, which explained why no one in the pack had found him. He knew Jesse could track their phones, but that didn't work if the battery was dead.

If they'd bothered to look for him at all.

Why should they? They could do without him. Jace was alpha, and although Rafe was Second, Jesse was the one who really helped with the day-to-day administration: organizing things, making alliances with other packs, negotiating deals. All Rafe contributed was labor—working up the mountain harvesting lumber, clearing land, building cabins. Anybody could do that.

He was just annoying everyone by being restless and unsettled. He'd been spending more and more time away from the pack since Jace brought Emma home. Not that he didn't like Emma—he liked her a lot. And unlike their Enforcer, Kane, and his shadow Israel, Rafe didn't

24

have a problem with their alpha taking a human woman as a mate.

It was just...they were so damn *happy*. The love between them was so palpable the rest of the pack could feel it. They basked in it like sunshine.

But it made Rafe feel...empty. Lonely. Like he didn't belong. He'd been riding Jace's coattails his whole life, and now Jace didn't really need him. No one did.

Feeling depressed, he packed up the angel's blankets and stored them back in their box. They still carried her scent—sweet and tantalizing. It confirmed she was a shifter wolf—the white wolf he'd seen just before his bike crashed. That was a surprise. As far as the Silverlake pack knew, there were no other wolves near their territory. And if she was caching supplies here, that meant she'd been in the area for a while. He held a fold of blanket to his nose and breathed her in. His mysterious angel had just gotten more mysterious, and more intriguing.

He shook his head, dropped the blanket and closed the lid of the box. Everyone called him an overgrown adolescent, but he didn't have to moon over a fantasy like he actually was one.

He packed up his stuff and got ready to make his way back to Silverlake. He was still debating whether to shift and go home cross-country, or go back down the road and try to hitch a ride. Or up to Grizzly's cabin and beg a ride home from the old bear.

He couldn't get the woman out of his mind, though. She was so breathtakingly beautiful, in wolf form and

25

human form. He vaguely remembered her smiling when he'd called her an angel. And...oh shit. He'd grabbed her breast. His face went hot at the thought. He might be a jackass by most people's standards, but he didn't go grabbing at women without an invitation.

Well. He had sort of an excuse—he'd been delirious at the time. But still, it was a dick move. Not good at all.

He wondered where the hell she'd come from—and where she'd gone. Part of him wanted to solve the mystery. The memory of her pulled at him—her face, the feel of her hands, the silkiness of her skin. She was like an itch he couldn't scratch.

Ah, well. He'd maybe look for her someday, thank her for what she'd done.

He was putting the last of his things in his bag when his wolf hearing picked up the sound of human voices. The pack? He went to the cave door and sniffed the air. No. Humans, and dogs. Hunters? He frowned. This was protected land. There was no hunting on it even in season, and this wasn't hunting season.

Something wasn't right. The men smelled— aggressive. Like they were looking for trouble.

Rafe made sure his gun was loaded, and then he pulled on the work pants and stuck the gun in the back of his waistband. He could protect himself better if he shifted, but if these men were hunting with dogs and rifles, wolf form was not the best way to go. Worst case, he'd end up shot; best case, he'd end up having to kill the dogs to get rid of them. And he liked dogs.

Shrugging on his shirt, he went outside. Right above

the cave entrance was a tumbled pile of boulders, with brush and scrub growing around them. He quickly climbed up and ducked behind them, in a place where he could watch the cave entrance and not be seen.

The men came crashing through the woods, lumbering like elephants to Rafe's ears. He waited while they followed the dogs up to the entrance to the cave. Then they deployed themselves like Secret Service agents, covering the entrance while two of them went in and checked the interior.

After a few minutes they came back out.

"Clear," one of them said. "There's nobody in there, although there was recently."

"What do we have?" another one asked. He was clearly the leader. A big man, dressed in camouflage like the rest of them, and carrying a hunting rifle. But they all also had handguns and radios. Not your typical hunting party.

The other one shrugged. "A fire—been out for a while. A little warmth in the embers. There's also a supply cache—food, first aid, extra clothes. And this." He tossed what remained of Rafe's bloody clothes down at the other man.

The leader frowned. "A fresh kill?"

The other man shrugged. "Maybe."

Someone else piped up. "Or maybe just an injured camper?"

"Hard to tell. Definitely not someone living there long-term, though."

"So if there's a camper, where are they?"

That was Rafe's cue. He stood up and cocked his gun so they could all hear it, and stepped partway out of his cover.

"Well, that would be me," he called down in a pleasant voice. "And I'm up here wondering why you nice gentlemen are nosing around my campsite with all those many weapons."

Instantly, he had six rifles trained on him. He stood his ground, weapon at the ready. The leader barked, "Come down from there."

Rafe gave the man his cockiest grin. "Seriously?" he asked. "I don't think so. See, up here I have cover. If it were necessary—which I hope it won't be—I could pick you off one by one from behind these rocks, while you would have a hell of a time trying to shoot me. Of course, you could take refuge in the cave, but then you'd be trapped."

The man kept his eyes on Rafe, clearly running scenarios in his head. He was obviously a professional. Military trained? Despite the cocky attitude he'd adopted, Rafe didn't like the looks of this at all.

Finally, the leader lowered his rifle. The others lowered theirs too—but not much.

"We have no beef with you," the leader said.

"So glad to hear it," Rafe said. "So, since this is a friendly chat and we're getting to know each other like the bros I know we'll be one day, I'll ask again. What the fuck are you doing here?"

The man's eyes narrowed, but he answered politely enough. "We're tracking a white wolf that's been seen in this part of the woods. Talked to some yahoos at a local bar who claim they saw a 'ghost wolf' on a stretch of road near here, couple of nights ago." He snorted. "Like it was a fucking harbinger of death or some shit. Said it killed some guy on a motorcycle. We found the crashed bike in a ravine off the road, but no body. So I guess the reports of his death were greatly exaggerated."

Not that exaggerated. Rafe knew that if he'd been human, he would have been dead. Even with his shifter abilities, he had the feeling it had been touch and go there for a while.

"Huh," he said to the man. "Pretty wild story, if you ask me. So you're like, animal ghostbusters? Cool."

The guy snorted again. "That wolf's no ghost. It's real, and we've been tasked to stop it."

That was wrong on a bunch of levels. Rafe raised his eyebrows. "Stop it from doing what? And tasked by whom, exactly? Notice how I used the word whom. It shows my education and knowledge. And one of the things I know is that hunting of all kinds is illegal on this land. I could tell you exactly how many laws you're breaking by bringing your dogs and your guns and your ghostbusters here, if you give me a minute to do the math."

He paused, then shook his head in mock regret. "Nope, sorry. Too big a number to add up in my head."

"The wolf's a killer," the guy said. "Killed some livestock, and possibly even a couple of people."

"By running their cars off the road?" Rafe asked. "Or by scaring them to death?"

"Mauling them," the man said.

Rafe raised his head and sniffed the air. He didn't even need the scent of the man's adrenalin to know that was a complete lie. He had a sudden uncomfortable feeling. Did they know the white wolf was a shifter? Was that why they were supposedly hunting an animal, and yet had approached the cave like there was a dangerous, intelligent human inside?

His insides went cold.

"Well, I haven't seen any wolves, ghosts or otherwise," he said. "And I've been here awhile."

"Really," the man said skeptically. "Just hanging out in this cave?"

"Living off the land," Rafe said. "See, I'm considering becoming a hermit. Like in those old stories? Gonna get me a brown robe and sit in my cave in silence. Contemplating. That is, if I can keep people from coming around and annoying me with guns and dogs and bullshit stories."

"A hermit," the hunter said. "That's cute."

"I know, right?" Rafe said. "So why don't you just leave me to my adorable contemplation, and then I won't have to shoot you, or even report you to the authorities for illegal hunting on protected land. Everybody wins."

They hesitated, and he tapped his gun on the rock meaningfully before aiming it once more at the leader. His voice went hard, and he channeled into it as much alpha energy he had. Not as much as Jace, but enough. "Don't make me ask you twice."

The dogs felt his inner authority, and began whining and pulling on their leashes—away from him. He could see the resolve of some of the men wavering, too. The leader was a human alpha, and not intimidated by Rafe, but he was smart enough to sense his men losing their desire for the hunt.

Once again Rafe could see the wheels turning in his mind, running scenarios, deciding whether to attack or retreat. Finally, he made a brief gesture to his men. They lowered their weapons.

"Enjoy your 'contemplation,'" the man said with a mock salute. "Hopefully, we won't see each other again."

"Likewise, I'm sure," Rafe said.

They backed up until they were out of handgun range, still watching him, as if he might really shoot them in the back as they left. Which told him what kind of men they were—the kind who would shoot you in the back with no warning, and assumed everyone was like them.

He watched them until they disappeared into the woods, then remained, scenting the air, until he was sure they were really gone.

He wondered why they were hunting the ghost wolf—his white angel. What had she done? Had she really killed a human? Why did she live as a lone wolf?

He'd been subconsciously debating whether to try to find her, or leave her as a beautiful fantasy in his mind. But she needed to be warned. He knew she wasn't the kind of killer that the hunters had claimed she was. She wouldn't have gone to all that trouble to rescue him if she was. And if she were a rogue wolf, it would be other shifters hunting her down. Not humans.

He went back into the cave, stripped, and packed the clothes into his saddlebags. If he was going to track the ghost wolf to her lair, he was better off doing it as a wolf.

The saddlebag had a special strap so that he could carry it in wolf form. He ducked his head into the loop and shook himself until the bag settled across his shoulders. Then he loped out of the cave and prepared to track his angel home.

CHAPTER 6

Terin was working in the garden outside her cabin. Normally she loved the orderly rows of herbs and vegetables, the feeling of the warm earth between her fingers, the smell of the growing plants. She loved her tidy cabin with its big double porch swing, and the hammock strung between two trees that was perfect for reading. She loved the quiet, with only the sounds of nature surrounding her.

But today it seemed too quiet. She couldn't stop thinking about the man in the cave. Was he all right? Had he woken up? Had she left him too soon, or had he healed and found his way home?

She let her fingers graze her breast. She couldn't stop thinking about the way she'd felt when he touched her. Not just the rush of heat, but the connection she'd felt to him. Almost as if she could feel what he was feeling—the bright places inside him and the broken places, and how they could be made whole.

When he'd thanked her, he'd gently taken her hand and kissed it. She could feel his lips on the tender skin of her wrist, the way he'd treated her like something precious. For a moment, she let herself wonder what it would be like to be with someone who treated her like that. But then she remembered how Ben had looked at her when he saw the monster in her, and was glad that she'd never have to see that look on the face of the man she'd rescued.

She'd started a new painting last night. A dark wolf, like she'd painted before. But he was surrounded by stars, and colors like the northern lights. She didn't know if the light was coming out of him, or funneling into him. It wasn't finished yet.

But she sensed her rescued wolf had colors inside.

She shook her head. She'd never know. All she would ever see of him would be on canvas.

She went back to her weeding, and then froze. She was being watched. There was a prickle beneath her shoulder blades, and the hair on the back of her neck was standing up.

Slowly she turned her head. At the edge of the forest, where it met the cleared land around her cabin, stood a huge black wolf. He blended into the shadows so well he would be almost invisible to someone without shifter vision.

Her mouth went dry. He was gorgeous, even more beautiful than her painting.

He stood motionless, staring at her, and she stared back. She knew who it was. She could feel him. But how had he found her? And why had he come looking?

As she watched, his body seemed to melt and rearrange itself. She was fascinated; she'd never seen someone change before. In moments, he was crouched on the ground in human form.

When he stood up she caught her breath. As beautiful as he was as a wolf, he was even more beautiful as a man. He was stark naked, bronzed, with that broad chest and those rippling abs, and long, strong legs. She couldn't keep her eyes from the nest of hair between his legs, where his thick cock rested.

She saw a flush come to his face, and he stepped behind a shrub, his carry bag in his hand. A few minutes later he came out, dressed, tucking in his shirt.

She sat, unmoving, as he walked across the yard to the edge of the garden, his eyes on her the whole way.

"You didn't have to do that," she said. Her voice felt husky from disuse. When was the last time she'd talked to anyone? "I've already seen you naked."

Oh, crap. The first thing she'd said to anyone in weeks, and it was about him being naked. What was wrong with her?

He didn't seem to mind, though. He shrugged, a grin curling the corner of his mouth. "You *do* talk."

"Not very often," she admitted. "Talking is overrated."

The grin deepened, and his eyes sparkled. "I've tried to tell that to many women in my time. Usually they don't believe me."

"Usually you're trying to get them into bed, I imagine," she said.

He looked unrepentant. "Well, yeah," he said, like it was obvious.

They fell silent, staring into each other's eyes.

Somehow Terin couldn't bring herself to look away, and it seemed like the man couldn't either.

She couldn't keep calling him 'the man,' though.

"What's your name?" she asked.

"Oh," he said, looking blank, as if it hadn't occurred to him she didn't know. "Rafe."

"Rafe," she repeated. "I'm Terin."

"Nice to meet you," he said politely.

She had to laugh. "It's a little late for 'nice to meet yous', I think," she said. "With me having already taken off your clothes."

Dammit, she was talking about nakedness again. He was going to get the wrong idea about her. But she couldn't seem to help herself.

"I know," he said. "Very forward of you." He paused, considering. "Although I'd let you do it again if you really wanted to."

Terin rolled her eyes. He was as incorrigible as she suspected. But then, she'd started the whole sexual innuendo thing, so she really couldn't blame him.

"I'll let you know if the urge comes over me," she said.

He smiled—a full-on smile—and she almost dropped her trowel. He had a gorgeous smile, hot and sweet and genuine. With more than a hint of bad boy underneath. Terin had a feeling that many of those women he'd referred to had seen that smile—and his abs—and decided that talking was overrated after all.

He broke eye contact with her, looking around the yard. "Do you live up here alone?"

"Yes," she said simply. "For years now."

He frowned, which bothered her. Like there was something wrong with that.

"I don't live with a pack, if that's what you mean," she said defensively. "I've never met another...someone like me."

He looked stunned at that. "Not ever?"

She shook her head.

His eyebrows drew together. "But—who raised you? I mean, you must have..."

"Parents?" she said. "Ah, no." She smiled mischievously at him. "I'm an angel descended from heaven, remember?"

He grinned at that. "Well, that explains it," he said. "But seriously, you must have come from somewhere."

She shrugged. It was something she'd given up thinking about a long time ago.

"I don't remember," she said. "I had an accident when I was sixteen. I don't remember anything that happened before that."

He dropped to the ground in one graceful movement and sat cross-legged. "Get out," he said. "Amnesia? For real?"

She nodded.

"Wow," he said. "That's rough. You've been alone all that time?" He sounded like it was completely unfathomable to him.

She shook her head. "There was a man—a human. He built this house. He was the one who found me and nursed me back to health. He was—he liked living off the grid. Anyway, we—he and I—"

"You fell in love," Rafe said softly.

Terin smiled sadly and looked down. "Something like that."

It was sweet that he was such a romantic. She wouldn't have thought it of him, with his reckless spirit and bad-boy attitude and sexual jokes. But he believed in love.

There was no way she could explain to him the complex tangle of caring and affection and need and dependence that had been her relationship with Ben. She'd cared about Ben, maybe even loved him in a way. And they gave each other companionship. But love like Rafe meant? She wasn't even sure she believed that existed.

She suddenly realized that the silence had stretched on way too long for most people to be comfortable with.

He was still sitting there, though, waiting, like he had all the time in the world. She said, "Why did you come here?"

He gazed at her, head tilted slightly to one side, eyes narrowed. Like he was trying to figure her out.

"First of all, I wanted to thank you for saving my life."

She shrugged, turning her face away, feeling uncomfortable. "I couldn't just leave you there, bleeding to death. Anyone would have done it."

"They would have called an ambulance, maybe," he said. "I seem to remember you going to a lot of trouble to haul me single-handed out of a ravine in the rain and save my sorry ass. Not to mention personally nursing me back to health."

She didn't say anything to that. She didn't know what to say—she didn't know what he wanted from her. Or how to talk to him. He didn't think they were going to have tea and chat, did he?

He didn't seem to mind her silence. He went on, "Mostly, though, I came because I wanted to warn you."

"Warn me?" she said. She'd lived on this mountain for years. What would he need to warn her about? "About what? I'm not infringing on your pack territory."

He looked shocked, and then a little embarrassed. "Oh, no, it's nothing like that," he said. "There's no territory dispute. But this morning, when I was leaving the cave, a group of human hunters came looking. For you."

Hunters? She flashed back for a moment, to the time she wanted to forget. Ben bringing a man dressed in hunting gear here. Because of her. She took a deep breath, trying to calm herself. That was years ago. And that man was gone. No need to panic.

She asked, "What kind of hunters?"

Rafe said, "The kind who said they were hunting a killer wolf, but acted like they were hunting for a person."

He let that sit while the implications sank into her mind. *Hunters who might know about shifters.*

He asked, "Do you know who they were?"

She shook her head helplessly. It couldn't be Ben's contacts—not after all this time. "I don't have any idea," she said.

Rafe was studying her. She was still trying not to panic. The memories always made her start to panic. And the thought of a group of hunters coming here—hell, the thought of being confronted with more than one person at a time—that made her panic too. She pushed down the wild fluttering sensation in her chest and breathed deeply, resisting the urge to change.

"Hey," Rafe said softly. He reached out, his fingertips grazing her arm. "Don't be scared. It'll be okay. Do you want to come back to Silverlake and stay with my pack until we can figure out who those guys are and get them off your trail?"

His pack. Lots and lots of wolves, people, all around her, wanting her to talk and socialize and do things, be with them. She started to hyperventilate. "No!"

He withdrew his hand and sat back, his voice still gentle. "Okay then, do you want me to stay with you?"

"No!" she choked out.

She looked at him. He was still watching her intently, but not with frustration or anger or annoyance. Just watching, as if he was trying to understand what she needed.

She closed her eyes and took a few deep breaths.

"It's okay," she whispered finally, over the lump in her throat. "I'll be fine."

"Okay," he said slowly, but he didn't look convinced.

Terin got her breathing under control. She wanted to change, to run—it was what she always did when she got panicked. But she wasn't going to. It was like his calmness was holding her here, making the feeling not so scary.

He sat without moving, just waiting for her to calm down. Strangely, she did. After a few minutes the panic began to fade. She thought of apologizing, but it was too many words. Too much explanation. And it didn't matter what he thought, really, did it?

They sat in the sun for a while, just breathing. Finally, the silence was broken by Rafe's stomach rumbling. He burst out laughing, and she found herself smiling as well.

"Sorry," he said. "I haven't eaten much for a couple of days."

"I know," she said. "It was all I could do to get enough tea down you to keep you hydrated."

"That was tea?" he said. "Huh. I thought it was wolf piss. That stuff was nasty."

She found herself throwing a weed at him. "It healed you, didn't it? You should be grateful."

His face sobered. "I am."

She looked into his eyes, at the light shining in them. Surprising herself, she said, "I was just about to have lunch. Would you like some?"

A slow smile spread across his face. "Yes, ma'am, I would," he said.

She stood up and led him into the house.

"What do you want to eat?" she called over her shoulder. "I have some chicken in the icebox. I could make sandwiches. Or you could have salad?" she asked dubiously.

He grinned. "I'm a wolf," he said. "Wolves eat rabbits, not rabbit food."

She smiled. "There actually is some rabbit in there," she said. "But vegetables are good for you. Vitamins and things."

He shook his head in mock amazement. "I wouldn't have thought you'd even know what vitamins were, what with amnesia and living all isolated up here."

She gave him a mock-stern look. "Watch yourself, buddy," she said. "I read a lot."

"I can see that."

As she put together some sandwiches, she could see him studying the open living/dining/kitchen area, as if he could learn about her by studying her habitat.

She tried to look at the cabin the way someone else would see it. The living area was large and sunny, with a shabby, comfortable sofa and chair. The walls were lined with bookshelves. She didn't have electricity, no phones or computers or television. She learned about the world by reading.

There was a small dining area, with a polished wooden table made out of a huge slice of tree trunk, and two chairs that Ben had made from gnarled tree branches. They gave the place kind of a fairy-tale look.

The kitchen was bright and pleasant, with cheerful curtains at the window over the sink. The sink itself had an old-fashioned hand pump, that brought up water from the well. There was no water heater—she heated all her water on the stove. There was a cold box in the corner that took blocks of ice. In the winter she and Ben had harvested them from the lake and stored them in sawdust in the underground ice house at the edge of the woods. Now she mostly got them from town. There were handmade wooden cupboards and shelves, filled with mismatched dishes. On display in the middle of one of the shelves was her favorite platter, an antique painted with an image of a lake on a starry night.

The cabin was simple, but she'd tried to make it pretty, with the curtains she'd sewn and the placemats she'd woven herself, and rag rugs she'd braided out of old clothes and fabric scraps.

It was comfortable. It was private. It was hers.

"I like your place," Rafe said finally.

She smiled because he sounded like he meant it, instead of just being polite. "Ben—my late husband—built most of it," she said, putting the plates down on the table. "He wasn't much for decorating, though. I did that."

"It looks nice," he said, taking a seat. "Homey. A lot better than my cabin at Silverlake. My decorating style is somewhere between bachelor pad and crack den."

She laughed. "You live by yourself?" she asked. She took a pitcher of lemonade out of the cold box and poured two glasses, bringing them to the table. She sat down.

He shook his head. "I share a cabin with Jesse. He and Jace and I—Jace is our alpha," he explained. When she didn't react, he said, "The head of our pack?"

She nodded, chewing slowly so she wouldn't have

to answer. She wished she could remember more about shifter packs. So he wouldn't think she was some kind of freak.

"Jace and Jesse and I have been friends ever since we were cubs," he said. "Then, when we were teenagers, our pack…"

He trailed off, a faraway look in his eyes. She could sense pain in him, an old pain, one that he usually covered up. "Our pack was broken up," he said. "Hardly any of us were left. Jace's dad—our old alpha—was gone, so Jace was alpha, but we had no home. No territory. No place to go."

Terin nodded sympathetically. "Like me, kind of," she said. "Except you weren't alone."

He looked up and smiled. "No," he said softly. "I wasn't alone." He was silent for a moment.

"Anyway," he went on, "we did everything we could to rebuild the pack. And finally, a few years ago, we were able to get Silverlake Mountain as our territory."

She watched his face, how it went soft when he talked about his friends, when he talked about the mountain. "It means a lot to you, doesn't it?" she said.

He frowned, as if trying to figure something out. "I thought it would mean more," he said slowly. "We worked for it for so long. It was all we could think about. And it was always the three of us. Then Kane and Israel found us, but they—well, they're pack, but I'm not close to them. Jace and Jesse are my brothers."

She watched him carefully, tuning in to that

connection she felt with him. "But something's wrong?"

His eyes grew dark, and then he shook off the mood he'd been in. "Nope," he said. "Nothing's wrong. Jace found a mate, a true mate, and sealed the magic on Silverlake Mountain. It's ours, and no one is going to take it away from us."

Terin was still watching him, trying to figure out how he really felt. He'd put on his lighter self like a bright-colored coat, but she could still feel the darkness beneath it. An old wound.

It made her want to reach out and touch him, to comfort him. He looked up and met her eyes, and she caught her breath. Something passed between them, some communication. Their gazes held for a long moment, until she couldn't handle the sense of closeness any more, and looked away.

After they finished eating, Rafe prowled around her space while she cleaned up, looking at her things, running his finger over the spines of her books. She felt like he was trying to see into her head through her belongings. She didn't know if she liked that or not.

It was exciting, in a way. To meet someone who wanted to know inside her. But it was scary, too, and she felt—invaded? She wasn't used to having someone in her space who paid so much attention to her.

The cabin felt smaller with him in it. When she'd lived here with Ben, it had just been home; it hadn't seemed small. But Rafe's presence filled it. She could almost feel the heat of his body across the room, and she was acutely aware of every movement he made. The shift of his leg muscles under his jeans; the way his chest muscles rippled under his shirt.

Suddenly she was having trouble breathing.

"I need to get some herbs from the garden," she said breathlessly.

She was out the door before he could answer, leaning against the wall of the house while she caught her breath.

He was so gorgeous. Hot, was what they said in the books she read. She felt like an idiot because she didn't even know how real people talked, what slang they used, or what kind of music was popular, or anything. She barely knew what was going on in the world off this mountain.

For the first time since she was a teenager, she wished she did. She wished she could be hip and amazing and fascinating and funny, and make him want to be with her.

Then she wished he'd go away and leave her in peace.

She went to the garden and pulled up some herbs randomly, just so she'd have something to take back into the house. But when she went back inside, he wasn't there. She glanced into the bedroom, but it was dim and still, her handmade quilt lying smooth on the bed. No wolf, no scent of one.

There was only one place he could be—and she didn't want him there. She hurried to her painting studio. It was a shed that Ben had built on the back of the cabin, with its own ventilation system, and insulated so that she could use it winter or summer. There was a heater for when the air got cold, kept way to the side, away from any flammable paint fumes.

He was standing at her easel, holding her unfinished painting by the edges. The black wolf under the sky full of northern lights.

No! He couldn't be in here. The paintings were part of her soul, and this was where she came to put the broken pieces of herself back together. No one was allowed in here.

Without thinking, she snapped, "Get out!"

CHAPTER 7

Rafe started at the sound of her voice, and almost dropped the painting. He'd been so entranced by it he hadn't even heard her coming. He looked up from the canvas. "This is—" he began.

"Don't touch that," she said sharply. "It's still wet. You could ruin it. And get out of here. I didn't say you could go wandering around my house, going through my private things."

Oops. Screwed up again. But the painting had drawn him in. "It's amazing," he said. "It's like—"

"Put. It. Down." She sounded as if she were trying very hard not to scream at him. "And get out of my space."

Whoa. Okay. He put the painting down carefully and stepped back. Then he walked out of the room, turning slightly to pass her without touching her. She looked like she was ready to change and attack him without warning.

He could almost hear her fuming. *How dare he invade her private space? Who did he think he was?* Rafe the fuck-up, as usual.

He stopped in the living room, waiting for her to

come out and say something to him. Yell at him. Anything. But she just walked past him, out the door, like she couldn't even look at him or talk to him.

He could understand her being upset, but there was more going on here. A few times she'd seemed on the verge of some kind of panic attack, like her wolf was going to burst out, or she was going to run. Something had happened to traumatize her, and his being here was messing with her head.

She stopped on the porch, holding on to the railing and breathing hard. He could sense her wanting to run, but she also probably didn't want to leave him alone in her house. She was really freaking out.

Well, he couldn't just stay in here. She needed something from him—even if it was nothing more than an apology. But he wanted to give her more. He wanted to heal whatever had hurt her. He could almost feel her panic in his own chest.

He wanted to barge out there in his usual impulsive way and try to fix it right away, but he knew he'd really blow it if he did that. He had to be patient, which he sucked at.

But he'd try.

Carefully, so as not to spook her, he walked out onto the porch and leaned against the railing next to her.

She stiffened up, but she didn't bolt. She didn't speak or look at him either, so on a scale of one to ten he figured he was at about a three.

"I'm sorry I looked at your paintings when you didn't want me to," he said quietly.

She didn't relax. Her hands were squeezing the railing in a death grip.

"You shouldn't have," she said. "You can't just go through people's private things without asking."

Damn. He kept forgetting what it was like for people who weren't in a pack. Emma was always yelling about privacy.

"I know," he said. "I forget, though. I'm used to the pack. Everybody's in each other's business and borrows each other's stuff. There's not a lot of privacy going on there."

"I'm not in your pack," she snapped.

Somehow, those words felt like they were piercing his chest. Like the branch that had impaled him, and almost as painful. He frowned, running his fingers up and down the porch support pole, wondering why she mattered to him so much.

"No," he agreed. "You're not." *But I wish you were.*

He sighed. "I shouldn't have gone in your studio. I'm too impulsive. Everyone says so." He paused, picking absently at a splinter in the wood. "It kind of goes along with talking too much. I don't stop to think. I'm sorry."

She bit her lip, and he could feel her begin to relax, her body not so tightly wound. He hoped she would believe that he hadn't meant to upset her. It almost killed him to wait in silence, instead of running his mouth as usual. But he couldn't rush her. She was like a wild animal, ready to shy away at the first wrong move. And for some reason, invading her studio had been a big one.

Finally her breathing steadied. Sounding a little surprised, she said, "You have a very calming presence."

That was the last thing Rafe had expected to hear. He burst out laughing.

"Me? I've been called a lot of things—most of them variations on 'obnoxious' and 'annoying,' he said. "Sometimes I'm amusing. Occasionally I'm even badass. But I'm pretty sure nobody in my whole life has called me 'calming' before."

She smiled a little. He loved to see her smile. He reached out his hand, hesitantly, and then smoothed his fingers gently up her forearm.

"Do you mind if I touch you?" he asked. She didn't object, so he stroked her gorgeous skin again, keeping the touch feather-light. "Most wolves find it comforting," he explained. "They need affection from their pack mates."

He saw goosebumps rise on her skin. Was she responding to him? Did she want him at all? Something inside him yearned for her, wanted to touch her and hold her and protect her. But if she told him to fuck off, he'd go. He didn't want to make her any more unhappy than she was. And he was not especially known for making people happy.

Only this time, he wanted to. He was shocked at how desperately he wanted it.

CHAPTER 8

Tingles were running up Terin's arm, and she was getting goosebumps. His hand was so warm. Just standing next to him made her want to snuggle up to him, feel his arms around her. It had been so long since she had been with a man. She wanted him to touch her more, but then she didn't know what the heck she would do with him after that.

She had the feeling he wouldn't just say thank you and go away.

She was afraid she wouldn't want him to go away. And then what would she do?

But she still found herself whispering, "I don't mind."

She angled herself slightly towards him. His hand went higher, skimming lightly up her arm and over her shoulder to cup her face. He moved towards her, slowly, giving her time to back off. Instead she shifted her body closer. She suddenly wanted to feel his lips on hers, to taste him, to feel his warmth spread through her.

He smiled slightly and tilted his head, brushing her lips gently with his.

Oh. That one tiny touch sent heat pulsing through

her. He returned his lips to hers, taking small sipping kisses. Terin raised her hands and slid them over his chest.

Rafe gathered her in his arms and pulled her close, fitting her along the length of his body. She could feel the hard muscles, her softness fitting perfectly against him. His cock was getting hard; she could feel it against her hips. The heat pooled between her legs, her insides going molten.

Terin was overwhelmed by the sensations. She deepened the kiss, sliding one hand up to tangle in his hair. It was soft and wild, just like she'd hoped it would feel. His tongue dipped between her lips and slid surely around hers, tasting her, tangling with hers, probing deeper. Terin felt a soft growl start in her chest. He felt so good, like luxuriating in the sun after a week of rain.

Without thinking, she slid her other hand around his waist and under his shirt, up the smooth planes of his back. The feel of his skin was intoxicating. He pulled her even more tightly against him, kissing her neck and across to her shoulder, gently closing his teeth on the sensitive place at the base of her neck before kissing it again. He kissed his way back up, lingering on her neck, making slow circles with his tongue just under her ear. Terin moaned, pressing herself against him. She felt him smile before he returned to her mouth and kissed her deeply once more.

His hand moved up her side, almost to her breast, and then he stopped, breaking the kiss and resting his forehead on hers.

"The first time I met you, I grabbed your breast without permission," he said. "I'd rather not make the same mistake again."

What was she doing? Terin felt a flutter of panic. Kissing was one thing. Breasts and other things… "I'm not—maybe we shouldn't—I mean—"

"Shh," he said, kissing her softly. "It's okay." He encircled her in his arms, relaxing against her. "God, Terin," he said. "You do something to me. From the first moment I saw you…"

"You were delirious," she reminded him, trying to catch her breath.

"Still am," he said. "Every time I see you."

"You've only seen me once. After the delirium, I mean."

He laughed raggedly. "Every time you go out of my sight, I hate it. And every time I see you again, it hits me just like the first time. Do you know how beautiful you are?"

She turned her head away, eyes down. "I'm not."

He slid his knuckle under her chin and lifted it, so that she looked him in the eyes.

"Why would you think that?" he said. "Your husband…he must have told you."

She stepped back, slowly. Rafe let his arms drop, but she could feel his reluctance to let go of her.

"Ben wasn't like that," she said. "It's not—he didn't—" She didn't know how to put it. She saw Rafe's eyes darken, and put a calming hand on his shoulder.

"He didn't hurt me or abuse me, if that's what

you're thinking," she said. "It's just—Ben was kind of a strange man. A loner. He moved out here because he didn't trust society or the government. He sort of thought everyone was out to get him. He wanted to be self-sufficient, live off the grid so that when everything went to hell, he'd be okay."

Rafe shook his head. "That's a little extreme, isn't it?"

Terin shrugged. "I guess it was, but for a long time I didn't know anything else. And he was kind to me."

Rafe sat down on the porch swing and pulled her down next to him. He stayed a few inches away from her, giving her space, but took her hand gently in his. "Tell me about him," he said.

She sat silently for a minute, wondering where to start. It was so hard to talk, especially about things that were important. Rafe didn't seem to be impatient, though. He just sat there beside her, waiting.

"He found me in the woods, when I was sixteen," she said softly. "Like I told you, I'd been in an accident, and I didn't remember anything from—before."

Rafe frowned. "Like, nothing? I mean, could you talk, and walk and everything?"

Terin nodded. "I had all my general knowledge, and skills," she said. "I just couldn't remember anything personal to me. Who I was, where my family was— nothing from my past. I didn't even remember my name, but I had some kind of ID card. Terin Whitney."

"But you don't know where you came from, or how you got here."

She shook her head. "Ben didn't know I was a shifter," she said. "I knew I was, I knew I could turn into a wolf, and I knew somehow that it wouldn't be good for him to know that. I was terrified he'd find out, in fact," she said. "So I hid it."

She thought back, to memories she hadn't allowed herself in years. "He was good to me, in his own way," she said. "He nursed me back to health. He said I was a skinny little thing, but he liked me fine," she added. "He didn't—I mean, he didn't force me to have sex with him or anything. At first, he just took care of me. I helped with the work, and the garden. I cooked. I could remember how to do all that—I just couldn't remember where I'd learned to do it. And when he found out I liked to read, he bought me books. And drawing materials, and paints. He wanted me to be happy," she said. "But he'd never take me into town unless I was dressed as a boy. He didn't trust anyone to know I was here."

Rafe frowned. "Didn't you want to go and look for your people?" he asked. "Find out who you were?"

Terin tried to think how to explain it. "I couldn't remember what had happened to me, but I remembered—fear," she said slowly. "Danger. It was just a feeling, but it was so strong. I felt like I had to stay hidden."

Rafe nodded slowly. "So you were okay with hiding up here?"

She nodded. "Over time," she said, "the two of us— well, a man and a woman alone together. We started into a relationship."

Rafe was stroking her hand with his thumb. "Did you love him?" he asked softly.

She was silent for a long moment. "I cared about him," she said finally. "I wasn't in love with him. I don't know if he was in love with me. But he was good to me, until…"

Rafe's hand grew still. "Until what?"

She shook her head. "I don't want to talk about that," she said. "He just kept getting more and more paranoid, until I was afraid of him."

They sat there for a long time in silence, Rafe holding her hand. Somehow, though, like before, the silence grew comfortable. Calming.

Then, without warning, a shot sounded in the woods. Far away, but they both started.

Terin looked at him. "It's probably just a poacher, hunting illegally," she said. "It happens all the time. Or someone shooting at a fox going after their hens."

Rafe's jaw clenched. "You didn't see those guys today," he said. "They were looking for you. They had dogs. If they pick up your trail and it leads here…"

"I can take care of myself," Terin said. "You don't have to worry about me."

Rafe shook his head. "But I will worry," he said. "This isn't random danger. They're targeting you. Why don't you just come back to Silverlake for a few days? Until I can find out who they are and what they're doing here?"

Terin tightened her lips. The thought of leaving

here, of being trapped in a place with all those people, touching each other and invading each other's privacy, made the panic rise in her chest.

"I can't," she said. "I have my garden. And my painting. I need that. I can't just go somewhere where I don't know anyone. Where there are all those people."

Rafe shifted on the seat so he could face her. "Then let me stay here."

She moved instinctively away from him. It was so tempting—to just throw herself into his arms and let him take care of everything.

But she couldn't do that. She couldn't give up everything she had and everything she was. She felt crowded, suddenly. Breathless. She was so attracted to him. But this was all happening to soon. Too fast.

"I can't," she said. "You don't understand. I just—it makes me feel—" She gave up in frustration. "I can't." She heard the panic in her own voice, and felt ridiculous.

Rafe's lips compressed. She could tell he was beating down his own urge to insist, to persuade her, to try to convince her. She felt her wolf clawing to the surface, wanting to run, to get away from this person who wanted things from her that she didn't know how to give him.

Who said he cared about her, but didn't know who she was or what she had done.

Rafe was silent for a minute. "Okay," he said quietly. "But can I come back and check up on you? Tomorrow?"

"I can take care of myself," she repeated stubbornly.

"Ben made sure of that."

He sighed. "I'm sure you can," he said. "But I'm still not happy about you being alone here. And since I'm unable to control my emotions—everyone says so—would you just humor my irrationality and let me come and see you?"

She hesitated, torn.

"You could make me lunch again," he said. "I'd let you do that."

Like he was doing her a favor. "Oh you would," she said. "Gosh, thanks. I suppose you'll let me do the dishes afterward, too."

"Sure," he said. "You don't think badasses like me do dishes, do you? At least, not without the right incentives."

"I bet," she said.

"So can I come?" His dark eyes were pleading.

She sighed. He was so damn irresistible. "Okay," she said. "If it makes you feel better."

He kissed her forehead. "Thanks," he said.

He left soon afterwards. She could tell by the way he slid his hand slowly from hers, until only their fingertips were touching, that he didn't want to go. But he'd said his pack would be worried about him, not having heard from him for so long.

She wondered what that was like, to have so many people wanting you to come home to them.

He stripped down and packed up his clothes, then shifted to wolf form and ducked his head through the strap of his saddlebags, letting them settle over his shoulders. She watched him leave from the front porch, and he paused at the edge of the forest, looking back at her.

She could feel how much he wanted to stay. Part of her wanted to call him back, to wrap herself in his arms and let him handle everything.

But she couldn't do that. She had to be strong. She had to take care of herself.

All the same, once he was out of sight, she shifted and ghosted after him, following his scent, wanting one last glimpse of him. She didn't know if he knew she was behind him. But when he reached the border of Silverlake territory, he stopped.

In the distance, she saw him turn and look back in her direction. He stood there for a long moment, and then turned and headed back to his own territory.

She doubted that he would come back. Once he was with his people, he'd feel different about her.

That thought made her feel lonelier than she'd felt in a long time.

CHAPTER 9

Rafe got a better homecoming than he'd expected.

Jace came bounding out of his cabin as soon as he heard Rafe arrive. He thumped Rafe on the back and pulled him into a bear hug, despite the fact that he was naked.

"Hey, man," he said. "Emma was worried sick about you. Where have you been? Why didn't you call?" He stood back and looked into Rafe's face, frowning. "You look like shit, man."

Rafe clapped him on the shoulder. "My buddy. Always making a guy feel like a million bucks."

Jace grinned, but it soon faded. "Really. You okay? Where's your bike? How come you're traveling four-legged?"

Jesse burst out of the cabin they shared, letting the screen door slam. "Is that Rafe?" he called. "Where the hell you been, deadbeat? I'm gonna kick your ass for making us worry like that."

Half the pack gathered around, everyone wanting to talk to Rafe, to touch him, to make sure he was okay. The feeling warmed him. He hadn't really thought they'd miss him so much. Of course, he was Second. But still…

"There's something going on," Rafe said to Jace, when he'd finished greeting everyone and exchanging friendly insults with the guys. "I need a meeting. You, Jesse, and I guess Kane and Israel better be in it too." He paused. "And Emma, of course."

"Emma better be included," she said, coming out of the cabin and giving him a big hug. "You jerk, you should have called!"

"Phone's dead," he said briefly. "And I ran into some trouble."

He looked meaningfully at Jace, who nodded.

"Somebody find Kane," he said to the people still milling around. "And Israel. Tell them to come to my cabin."

Everyone began to wander back to what they'd been doing, and Jace led the way into the cabin. Rafe dug the pants Terin had given him out of his bag and put them on, and shrugged into the work shirt without bothering to button it.

Emma had given him one considering look and then gone into the kitchen and started putting a plate of food together. "Are you sure you're all right?" she asked, handing him a sandwich.

Rafe nodded. "I crashed my bike and got busted up pretty bad," he said around mouthfuls of bread and meatloaf. He couldn't believe he was hungry again. Healing took a lot of fuel.

"God, Emma, this is great." He added, "It took me all this time to heal. I'll tell you the story when everyone gets here."

Jace nodded, and waited for the others. Rafe continued to chow down until they got there, building up his strength. After a few minutes Kane walked in, huge and stone-faced as usual. His shadow Israel trailed silently behind him—also as usual. Israel uttered like maybe three words a week. Both of them irritated Rafe. They were good fighters, good at security, but nobody could ever tell what the hell they were really thinking. Except they obviously thought that nobody besides the two of them was worth talking to.

When everyone was settled around the dining table, Jace passed around beers and Rafe started his story.

He told them the whole thing, from the bar fight to the crash, to Terin's rescue and meeting the hunters, and then finding Terin's cabin.

Jace's face grew more and more concerned as he took in the information about Terin and the hunters. "They were looking for this woman specifically?" he said. "But they weren't ordinary hunters?"

Rafe shook his head. "They said they were hunting a wolf, but the way they tracked her, the way they entered the cave—it was like a military unit on an operation, where they expected the person they were tracking might have a weapon. They weren't approaching it at all like a hunt for an animal."

"So they probably knew she was a shifter," Jesse said. Everybody looked edgy at that. Heavily armed hunters who knew about shifters could be very bad news. "Were any of them shifters?"

"No," Rafe said. "All completely human. Which is what bothers me the most. Who were they? How did they know about Terin, and why were they after her?"

"And how did they know she was in this particular area?" Kane added. "They didn't track her straight to the cave from somewhere else—you said you'd been there a couple of days when they showed up."

Rafe nodded. "They said that the guys who chased me were telling everyone they'd seen a ghost wolf."

There were snorts and eye rolls at that.

"So the hunters have been canvassing the area, picking up rumors," said Kane. "But what brought them here in the first place? Who knows about shifters and would have sent them here?"

Jace and Emma exchanged a glance. "Not Alexander Grant, I hope," Jace said.

Rafe hoped not too. Grant was Emma's psycho ex. She'd been on the run from him when she and Jace met, with some evidence that could hopefully bring down his criminal empire. The FBI was working on it, but as of now the evil empire was still standing. And Grant was pretty pissed off at the Silverlake pack. Especially at Jace, who'd clawed up Grant's pretty-boy face when the douchebag had tried to kill Emma.

"Do you think?" Emma was saying. "But why would he go after this Terin? He can't use her against us—we didn't even know she existed."

Jace shook his head. "I don't know which idea I like less," he said. "That Alexander Grant is targeting shifters, or that someone in addition to Grant knows about us and is targeting shifters."

Yeah, Rafe thought. *Either possibility sucks.*

Israel murmured something to Kane, who nodded. "It's possible that it's someone from Terin's past," Kane pointed out. "She may have been running from someone when she ended up in these mountains in the first place. Did she ever try to find out who her people were, or where she was from?"

Rafe shrugged. "Not that I know of," he said.

"So there could be any kind of trouble following her," Kane said, glancing pointedly at Emma. She raised her eyebrows at him. Kane hadn't been happy about Emma mating with Jace, and, as the pack's Enforcer and head of security, he *really* hadn't been happy about having to defend the pack from her evil ex and his security forces.

Jace said, "Kane, go back down to that bar Rafe was drinking at and see if you can track down the hunting party, or the guys who told them about the white wolf. Find out everything you can about how and when those hunters showed up, and where they might be from."

Kane gave a curt nod, glaring at Rafe like all this was his fault.

Rafe ignored him. Turning to Jace, he said, "I'm trying to convince Terin to come here. She's not safe at that cabin on her own. They could track her there, if their dogs are good enough. I did it."

Jace said slowly, "I suppose she could come here, if she wants to."

Emma gave Jace a *'what's wrong with you'* look. "Of

course she can. She must be really scared, all by herself, with no pack. You should have brought her back with you."

Rafe sighed. "Do you think I didn't try?" he asked. "She wouldn't come. She's terrified of people. She's been alone there so long, and I think something bad happened to her when her husband died."

Kane muttered, "Oh, great. A trauma queen."

Rafe continued to ignore him. It was really the only way of dealing with Kane, except for smacking the shit out of him, which he preferred not to try and do in his half-healed condition.

"If she won't come here, I'm going to have to go back there and at least see if she'll let me stay with her," he said. He turned to Jace. "Can I have some troops to help me out, in case those guys show up again?"

Kane frowned. "Wait a minute," he said. "It's bad enough taking her in, if this militia group is after her. Did you all learn nothing from the Alexander Grant disaster?"

Emma gave him a slitty-eyed glare this time, which Kane ignored.

He went on, "I can't stop you from bringing her here, and of course my people will defend the perimeter of our territory regardless of the source of the threat. But as head of security for this pack, I have to say that it's fucking stupid to jeopardize our territory by pulling our defense team and sending them into a probable military action to protect a non-pack member who doesn't even want to be protected."

Rafe's wolf felt like it was going to burst out of his chest and rip Kane's throat out. What the hell was the matter with that guy? Terin *had* to be protected, at all costs.

He growled, deep in his chest. "Don't you get it?" he snarled, rising out of his chair. "She's scared of people. She's been traumatized—maybe more than once. But we have to protect her. If anything happens to her—" He moved in on Kane, who also rose to his feet. Both of them were growling now.

"Jace?" Emma said faintly. "What's going on?"

It was Israel the silent who finally spoke. "Oh, fuck," he muttered to Kane. "She's his mate."

Everyone stared at Rafe. Kane raised his eyes to the ceiling, shaking his head in despair.

"Is she?" asked Jace.

"I—she—we haven't—we just met—" Rafe stammered to a halt. Oh, shit. Was that what this feeling was? Somehow he'd thought that finding a true mate was supposed to feel better than this.

Jesse clapped Rafe on the shoulder. "Judging by the look on your face, I think she is," he said. "But I'm guessing she doesn't know it yet."

"Oh, for fuck's sake," Kane said. "Another 'fated mate'? When are you people going to get rid of these antiquated notions about magic and true love?"

He put his hands on his hips and stared at Rafe. "Look at you," he said. "You're a mess, over a woman you've known for two days and who's an emotional train wreck, to hear you tell it. We're a small, new pack, and we need to move forward making rational, strategic mating and trade decisions that bring us beneficial alliances. We need to start thinking, to use our heads instead of basing all our decisions on overblown emotions. Remember what happened with our old pack?"

He looked around the room. "Am I the only one who remembers that we were decimated because certain people couldn't manage to keep their fucking pants on?"

Jace pushed back his chair and rose slowly to his feet. "That's my family you're talking about," he said in a low, deadly voice. "Watch yourself."

Kane refused to back down. He snarled, "We need to build a strong pack, not a camp for fugitives and refugees. How the hell am I supposed to do my job if I have to trail around behind a string of guys who can't think with anything but their dicks?"

That was it. Rafe lunged at Kane, growling. Jesse grabbed him, hauling him back. Kane snarled again.

Jace slammed his hand on the table. "That's enough!" His voice thundered through the room, backed by his alpha energy. Rafe shook Jesse's grip off him, panting. Kane had frozen in place, but his chest was still out, his stance aggressive.

Jace said dangerously, "Are you challenging me, Kane?"

Jesse chimed in quietly, "Okay, now, this is fun and everything, but let's not tear Emma and Jace's kitchen apart rolling around in a fight like cubs," he said.

Jace and Kane were still staring at each other, eyes

burning gold. Emma was staying very quiet, which Rafe thought was a good plan for someone who couldn't turn into a wolf if things got crazy.

Rafe moved to stand shoulder to shoulder with Jace, and Israel had risen and come up behind Kane's left shoulder.

Jesse shook his head. "Boys, boys, boys," he said. "Talk about not thinking before you act. How's a Mexican standoff going to solve anything?"

"It's not going to be a standoff much longer," Rafe said, his wolf panting to get out. "I'm planning on beating the shit out of Kane."

Jesse said, "Because that will make him more willing to protect your mate?"

Kane probably wouldn't protect Terin anyway, unless Jace ordered him to. But Jesse was right; he definitely wouldn't if Rafe beat the shit out of him. He let out a huge breath.

Jace and Kane had been ignoring him in any case, staring each other down. Figured. Again, Rafe was not needed.

Jace and Kane stared at each other a moment longer, and then they both sat back down. You couldn't say they relaxed, exactly, but the Defcon threat alert went down a level.

"So let's consider Rafe's request," Jesse went on, as if they had all been sitting there comfortably sipping beer the whole time.

As usually happened when Jesse took control of a tense situation, Rafe found his anger being defused, his wolf retreating and his brain engaging. He could see it happening to everyone else, too. Nobody knew how Jesse did it. It was his superpower.

"Okay," Jesse said. He put on his negotiator persona, which he used when dealing with other packs. "Kane is correct, in that deploying an unknown number of troops outside our territory for an unknown period of time, for a threat that involves serious firearms, is probably not the best plan."

"Fucking stupid," Kane muttered again.

Jesse didn't even look at him, just proceeded in outlining the situation. Since smacking the shit out of people seemed to be off the table for the moment, Jesse had apparently concluded that ignoring Kane was the only option left.

Jesse went on, "Were we to extend an official offer of sanctuary, the wolf in question—Terin, you said her name was?"

Rafe nodded briefly.

"Okay. Terin could choose to come here."

Rafe opened his mouth, and Jesse held up his hand. "Yeah, I get it, bro. She doesn't want to. But she's a grown woman, and unfortunately you can't decide for her what she wants to do. If she wants to take her chances in her cabin, there's not much you can do unless you decide to kidnap her."

Israel was watching Rafe's face. "Oh, geez, he's thinking about it," he mumbled.

Rafe didn't say anything. He was busy trying to figure out if that would work, and if Terin would ever forgive him if he tried.

"Oh, for fuck's sake," Kane said. "I'm done here."

He pushed back his chair and stood up, turning to Jace, his whole demeanor stiff and formal to the point of mockery. "With your permission, *alpha*, I'll go take care of my original mission, which is to determine the nature and imminence of the potential threat."

Kane glanced at Rafe, and then said, "I'm also going to do a background check on this Terin Whitney and find out where she comes from, and who might be after her. Even though no one had the sense to ask me to."

He turned and stalked out, Israel following.

There was a brief silence.

"Well," Emma said. "That went well."

Rafe put his head in his hands. "Shit. This is such a mess." He didn't know what to do. His wolf was all for the 'kidnap Terin' idea, but that was clearly a bad idea. Probably.

Jace said, "If you are accepting that this woman is your mate, then she's your responsibility until and unless she agrees to join the pack. She's welcome to our protection if she wants to come here, but if she insists on staying alone…"

"Women," Rafe muttered. "Why are women so damned stubborn? Is it an X-chromosome thing?"

Emma snorted. "Yeah, like people with Y-chromosomes are immune to stubbornness. Not."

Jesse said to Rafe, "Maybe Jace and Emma could go talk to Terin with you. Officially extend the pack's invitation of sanctuary." He turned to Jace. "She might feel more comfortable if she actually met you. And you can also assess how likely she is to bond with the pack, and whether—ah—she's likely to fit in."

"Meaning, is she a nutcase," Rafe said. "That was really not as subtle as you thought it was, Jess."

He hadn't even considered that the pack might not want Terin. That couldn't happen. They couldn't reject her. He didn't know how, but he knew that would break her forever.

"Sorry," Jesse said.

"What's she like, Rafe?" Emma asked.

He tried to think how to explain Terin. "She's beautiful," he said, knowing how inadequate that was. "Strong and fragile at the same time. And she's an amazing artist. Her paintings…" he trailed off, unable to put the power of her paintings into words. "I don't know everything she's been through," he said, "but she's not crazy. She's survived all on her own, and she's brave and funny and…" He choked up and couldn't continue.

Jesse said, "We're with you, bro. If there's anything I can do…"

Rafe thumped him on the shoulder. Then he turned to his alpha. "Jace, I can't just let her get killed because of fear and stubbornness. I have to protect her, even if I have to do it on my own."

"I know," Jace said quietly.

Rafe shook his head, frustrated. "No you don't. When you and Emma needed help, you had the whole pack behind you. All of us, ready to come to your rescue—to do anything you wanted or needed."

"This isn't the same—" Jace started.

Rafe said, "No. It's not. Because it's me, not you. Everyone here would do anything for you, but I'm just Rafe the fuckup. Nobody's coming to my rescue. Or my mate's. I have to do it myself."

He shoved back his chair, which tipped over and crashed to the floor. Without even stopping to pick it up, he stomped out in Kane's wake.

After his dramatic exit, Rafe was full of restless energy that he didn't know what to do with. This was when he usually picked a fight with someone, or went out and did something crazy on his bike. But he didn't have his bike and he was too beat-up for a fight. And he couldn't afford to do that stuff now, anyway, not with Terin in danger.

He didn't want to talk to anyone in this state, so there was nowhere to go but his cabin. He couldn't help but feel how ironic it was that he couldn't seek comfort with Terin. He was going through all this, driving himself crazy and alienating his pack leaders, for a woman who probably didn't even want him.

He walked through Jesse's neat and tidy side of the cabin, into his own messy disaster of a room. The cleaning fairy hadn't made a surprise visit since he'd left, and so he just upended his saddlebags and dumped everything on the floor with the rest of his crap.

He flung himself on the bed—which was really just a mattress on the floor—and stared moodily at the ceiling. He was struck by the contrast between his place and Terin's cozy cabin, which reflected her personality so clearly. He didn't want to think about what his living space said about him.

His sharp hearing picked up voices outside. Jesse and Jace. "Kane's just getting worse," Jesse was saying. "More ambitious, and less willing to consider the feelings and needs of individual pack members. If we're not careful, he'll have us all making strategic mating contracts, just to gather more territory and influence. Which we don't even want."

"I know," Jace said with a sigh. "What he really needs is a mate of his own."

Rafe could almost hear Jesse rolling his eyes. "I can't even imagine who'd put up with Sir Stick-Up-His-Ass," he said. "Whoever that poor hapless wolf girl was, we'd have to stop the mating just out of mercy to her."

Jace said, "He has the best interests of the pack at heart."

Rafe heard Jesse snort. He and Kane had never gotten along—not since they were cubs.

Footsteps came into the cabin. From the sound, Rafe knew it was Jace, not Jesse. Rafe stayed where he was, flopped on the bed.

Jace came in and leaned against the doorframe. "Forgot to pay the cleaning lady again, I see."

"Shut the fuck up," Rafe said, but without animosity.

"Look," Jace said. "I know how you feel. When I first met Emma, I had no idea how to convince her to be my mate. How much I needed her," he added.

Rafe didn't say anything. Jace didn't get it. No one did.

"But the thing is, if she's your true mate, she needs you, too," Jace said. "Trust her. She'll figure it out."

"If she doesn't get killed first," Rafe said. "Without me there to protect her."

Jace came and dropped down on the side of the mattress. "I know it's hard," he said. "Like your whole world suddenly tilted on its axis. Everything changes overnight, and you're left with your heart torn wide open, vulnerable to someone who's not on the same timeline you're on."

Nailed it. Unfortunately, happy-ever-after Jace perfectly describing the pain in Rafe's heart wasn't especially comforting.

"I need to *do* something, or I'll fucking explode," Rafe said. "How the hell am I, of all people, supposed to bond with a woman who needs an unending supply of patience? I have the patience of a gnat."

Jace grinned. "You'll figure it out."

Rafe shook his head. "Who are you trying to kid? Hell, who am *I* trying to kid? I'm going to suck at this. Even if she doesn't get herself killed, I can't make her happy."

"I think the same thing every day," Jace said.

Rafe rolled over and looked at him. "You're nuts," he said. "Emma adores you."

His alpha shook his head, looking bemused. "Yeah. And every day I'm afraid she's going to find out how

75

much I suck and stop," he said. "But all I can do is keep trying. Keep loving her. Keep saying I'm sorry if I fuck up. And keep reminding myself that somehow, for some reason, she does need me."

"That doesn't actually sound that fun," Rafe said grumpily.

"It's awesome," Jace said, a sappy look coming over his face. "You'll see."

Rafe grunted.

Jace thumped him companionably on the chest. "Why don't we do what Jesse suggested?" Jace said. "I'd like to meet Terin. Emma and I can come with you, talk to her. I can get an idea of how she would respond to the pack bond."

"And if she doesn't?" Rafe said. "Respond to the pack bond, I mean."

"I don't know," Jace said. "But one thing at a time, okay? Just let us meet her."

Rafe considered, biting his lips. It wasn't like he had much of a choice.

"Okay," he said. "But I don't want to blindside her. I'll go over first, tomorrow morning, and see if I can persuade her to at least meet with you. Once I sound her out, I'll call you and let you know."

Jace said, "That sounds fair." He paused, then said, "Rafe, bro, I'm behind you on this. But I also have the whole pack to think of. I have to protect them."

Rafe looked away. "I can't do this alone, Jace."

Jace sighed. "We'll do everything we can to make sure she's safe. I give you my word."

CHAPTER 10

The next day, Terin decided that she had to save herself.

She'd stayed up all night, trying to read, with a rifle next to her chair. She'd told herself that she was being vigilant, not scared. A few times she nodded off, only to have a small sound jerk her awake, heart pounding.

The men with the guns didn't come. Neither did Rafe.

She reminded herself she hadn't expected him to come back last night. He'd said he'd come today. Besides, he was still healing, and he'd been away from his pack—his family—for two days. They probably wanted to spend time with him. And he had to find his crashed motorcycle and try to save it.

But deep inside, she believed he probably wouldn't come back at all.

And if Rafe wasn't coming back, then she would have to defend herself. She knew how. Ben had been convinced that government agents were going to show up at any moment to try to take him away.

So he'd taken precautions to make sure they didn't.

He'd set up traps around the perimeter of the property. Concealed pits, some with sharpened stakes in the bottoms. Trip wires, net traps—plenty of ways to keep people out, or to neutralize them once they were in.

These were things she hadn't explained to Rafe. She hadn't had the words to explain. It was the traps that had done Ben in, and Terin hadn't maintained them since he'd died. She had never believed anyone was after her, once the man Ben brought here was gone. But now that she knew someone was, she silently thanked Ben for his paranoia.

And she prepared her traps.

But she still couldn't put Rafe out of her mind. She thought about what a luxury it would be, to have someone sweep into your life and take care of everything. But then, what happened if they got tired of taking care of you? What happened if it got to be too much? Or if they got sick, or hurt, or died?

She'd counted on Ben. Ben had promised her he'd always take care of her and protect her. But Ben had changed—and then he'd died. Even though he wanted to keep his promise, he couldn't.

So why would Rafe be different? Rafe said himself that he was irresponsible, that everyone in the pack called him a fuck-up.

She'd felt how much he cared about her. How much he wanted to help her.

She just didn't know if she could trust him to keep caring.

She closed her eyes and relived the feeling of his hands on her body—the way he'd kissed her. The passion, the heat. How gentle he'd been with her, how patient, when all the time she could sense how wild he was underneath.

How much he wanted her.

She wanted him too. Her body yearned for him, wanting to wrap itself around him and soak in his scent, his heat. To feel his throbbing cock inside her, stroking her until she cried out and felt her orgasm shatter around her.

But she was the real fuck-up. Beyond that, she was cursed. Dangerous. And he would see that and he would leave her, and then she would be even more broken. So broken she'd never heal.

But she still wanted him.

She went into the house and baked a pie for lunch. Just in case he came back.

And then she went back to setting her traps. Just in case he didn't.

CHAPTER 11

Rafe drove his truck up to Terin's cabin. The door was propped open, and clean laundry was hanging on the clothesline, fluttering in the slight breeze.

He got out of the truck, leaning on the open door, and sniffed the air. He couldn't get a fix on Terin. This was her place—her scent was everywhere.

"Terin?" he called out. "It's Rafe. I just wanted to see if you're okay."

Silence. A chicken squawked inside its coop, and there was the low buzzing of insects in the grass. The place looked peaceful in the sunlight. Like somewhere you could sprawl out with a beer and just chill. Where you didn't have to worry about anything but tending the garden and feeding the chickens. Or eating them.

When Terin didn't appear, Rafe went up to the house and knocked on the open door.

"Terin?"

There was still no answer, and the house felt— empty. Still, he went inside and checked. He was starting to get worried, even though he knew there was no reason. There was no scent of the men and dogs he'd encountered—no scent of anyone who shouldn't have been here.

But there was no Terin, either.

Despite himself, he peeked into her studio again. She'd done more work on the painting. The dark wolf.

He was sitting on a mountaintop, nose raised to the wind. He looked lonely, and yet the bright colors in the sky seemed full of hope. It took Rafe a minute to realize that another wolf had been added to the scene. Hidden in the trees near the bottom was a pale wolf. Watching. And every line of her body spoke with longing.

He stared at it for a long time, wondering what it meant. Hoping it meant she felt something for him. Then he turned away and went back out of the house.

Where was she? Had she gone for a run in the woods? That was crazy. What if she ran into the hunters? He knew he shouldn't worry so much, but he couldn't help it.

He walked around the perimeter of the property, where the woods surrounded the sunny clearing. Something was bothering him—small changes in the landscape that his wolf was processing on a subconscious level. He couldn't have said exactly what they were, but he felt a prickle along the back of his neck, like there was danger nearby.

Then he saw her. She was at the edge of the woods, watching him, just like the wolf in the painting. He couldn't help but smile when he saw her, and he felt his shoulders relax in relief.

"There you are," he said. "I couldn't find you."

She just looked at him, staying in wolf form. As if

she didn't want to talk to him.

He began to get a little annoyed. "You scared me," he said. "I was afraid those hunters had met you in the woods and—and taken you." He couldn't bring himself to say 'killed.' Ever since he'd realized she was his mate, the thought of losing her felt like he'd swallowed ground-up glass.

"You need be more careful," he went on, hearing himself sounding like an overprotective chauvinistic ass, but somehow unable to stop talking. "Look how open this place is. A million ways to get in. At least stay near the house."

Her head had gone up as he was talking, and she gave a soft growl.

"Come on, don't be like that," Rafe said. "You know I'm right."

Shut up, shut up! he was telling himself. But his mouth just kept moving. "It's why we form packs. Why won't you at least think about coming back to Silverlake with me? You might like it there. And it would be safer than here."

He was walking forward as he spoke, eyes on her. She backed up, still watching him, her tongue out now. As if she'd stopped being pissed and started laughing at him.

"Fine, then," he said. "I'll have to protect you here."

She gave herself a shake, as if he were water she wanted to get off her hide.

"Oh, really?" he said. "I'll have you know that I'm Jace's Second, and I've been in plenty of fights. Won

82

most of them, too. And I can shoot. And I can—"

He took another step forward, and suddenly felt a tug at his feet. Before he could move, a loop of rope wrapped tight around his ankles. He heard a loud 'snap' and then he was dragged upwards, feet first, hanging upside down from a tree.

You've got to be fucking kidding me.

He found himself twirling slowly, like a mobile over a kid's crib. He kept trying to lift up his upper body so he could reach his ankles and free himself, but each movement sent him spinning dizzily. After a minute he realized he probably didn't want to free his ankles, because it would mean falling headfirst about fifteen feet. Probably not fatal, unless he broke his neck. He swam his hands through the air, making himself rotate until he could see Terin.

She was still in wolf form, sitting on her haunches. Her head was cocked and her tongue was hanging out the side of her mouth.

Damn, she *was* laughing at him.

"Okay," he said. "Very funny. You can protect yourself. I take it all back. Just get me the hell down from here."

She sat for another minute, then slowly got up, stretched, and changed back to human.

Rafe's mouth went dry. Even hanging upside down, feeling like a complete and total ass, the sight of her naked made him crazy.

She was so beautiful. Her lightly bronzed skin, with no tan lines, and that pale, pale hair sweeping down her back. He could close his eyes and remember the way it felt like silk running through his hands. He wanted to take her ripe breasts in his mouth, one at a time, and kiss and caress them until she was wet and moaning. And then he wanted to...

Terin released some kind of catch on the back of the tree, and Rafe plummeted to the ground. He put his hands over his head to break his fall, so he didn't in fact break his neck, but the landing gave him a serious jolt.

She stood, arms across her chest, while he disentangled himself from the rope. "Now I'm going to have to reset this one," she complained.

Rafe rubbed his ankles to restore the circulation. "You have more than one of those?" he asked.

"Did you think I was totally defenseless? Oh, wait, you did. That's what that lecture was all about."

He rose to his feet, brushing himself off. "No offense, but you do look kind of defenseless. It's deceiving."

She turned away, but not before he saw the hint of a smile on her face. "Well, I'm not."

He knew he should think of a clever reply, but he couldn't seem to. He was looking at her perfect ass, and that was pulling all the blood from his brain and sending it straight to his cock. All he could think of was kneeling her down and burying himself inside her, taking her from behind and hearing her moan and growl like the gorgeous wolf she was.

"Um...yeah," he managed to say.

She turned around, quick enough that he couldn't

avert his gaze. Hers shot to his cock, which was straining against his jeans.

"I thought you came because you wanted to protect me."

"That too," he said, before he thought. He sighed. This was not going well. "It would be a lot easier to focus on that if you had clothes on, though. Just sayin'."

She finished resetting the trap, laying out the rope loop and covering it with dirt and leaves, and resetting the trip wire. He examined it—it was pretty ingenious.

"Did you think this up?" he asked.

She shook her head. "No. Ben did. My husband."

"Holy hell," Rafe said. "He really was paranoid, wasn't he?"

"I told you," she said. "He thought government agents were going to come along and take everything away from us. He didn't trust them."

"What about you?" Rafe said. "Do you not trust them either?"

She gave him a sidelong glance. "I don't trust anyone."

Rafe heaved another sigh. It figured.

She began walking toward the house, and he followed her, appreciating the view. At least she hadn't kicked him off her land yet. That was something.

He circled around to catch up with her, and she said, "Watch out, there's another trip wire."

He barely managed to avoid it.

"Stick close to me," she said. "If you're good, I'll show you where they all are later."

"I'm very good," Rafe said. "Ask anyone that I've ever—"

She shot him a raised-eyebrow look.

"—slept with," he finished lamely, before he could turn his mouth off. *Nice, Rafe. Very romantic. Tell her about all your happy booty babes.*

Shit.

She walked into the house, not inviting him inside. On the other hand, she didn't tell him *not* to come in, so he followed her. She reached over to a peg near the door, snagged a long cotton skirt, and stepped into it, shimmying it up over her hips in a way that made Rafe want to tear it right back off. Then she pulled on a tank top, covering those incredible tits.

Rafe didn't know whether to be disappointed or relieved.

She shook out her hair in a gorgeous shimmer, and then turned to face him. "So," she said, "Why did you come back?"

He looked at her, confused. "I said I would," he told her. "I couldn't just leave you here alone."

She looked directly at him. "Why not?"

Rafe didn't know what to say. *Because you're my mate,* he wanted to say. *Because I think I love you.* But he couldn't tell her that. He'd scare her off.

"You didn't leave me after I crashed my bike," he said instead. "You carried me all the way to that cave. You healed me. You brought me food and clothes. You didn't have to do all that. But you did. Why did *you* help *me*?"

She looked back at him, her blue eyes fathomless. "I'm not a monster," she said softly. "Anyone would have tried to help."

"So why can't you believe that anyone would want to try to help you?"

She looked away. "People say they want to help. And then...things happen."

Rafe stood there, trying to think of what else to say. She had so many secrets she didn't want to share. How could he figure out what she needed if he didn't know what was wrong?

Finally he said, "Look, I don't know what's happened to you in your life. I know it's been hard, and there haven't been many people you can count on. Maybe one. Maybe none."

She looked away, biting her lip.

"And sure, I'd like to tell you that you can always count on me. That I'm chock-full of responsibility. But that would be Jace, my alpha. Or that I'm the guy who always keeps a cool head, who's steady and dependable and can defuse a potential war in ten minutes flat. But that's my bro, Jesse. Or even that I always do the right thing, even if I have to shove a major stick up my ass to do it. But that would be Kane, our Enforcer."

She smiled at his description of Kane. Well, at least he could amuse her. That was a start.

"And then there's Israel, Kane's shadow." He considered. "You'd probably like him. He doesn't talk either."

No, wait, he didn't want that. "No, don't like him,"

Rafe said. "Forget I even told you about him. You should like me."

That got him another smile. Progress.

"The truth is, I do two things well," he said. "Fight, and make people laugh. So maybe that's all I can offer you—a little entertainment until these guys come after you and I kick their asses."

He moved forward, slowly, not wanting to spook her.

"I'm not saying I'm any prize," he admitted. "I don't think anyone in my pack would say I am. But I love the people I love, and I'd do anything for them. And I wish..." he broke off, and she tilted her head, watching him, waiting for him to go on. "I just wish you'd let me stay here with you," he said. "Even if you don't need it. And maybe—maybe I can do this one thing right."

He looked away. He hadn't meant to say that last part. But she closed the space between them, her hand on his arm light as a butterfly.

"Don't say that," she said. "I think you're better than that. I think you're a good man."

He grinned at her. "I wouldn't go that far. For instance, I can't stop thinking about you naked."

That brought a smile that lit up her eyes and took his breath away.

"I guess you can stay around if you want to. For a while," she said. Her eyes glinted wickedly. "I'll protect you."

She tilted her head up and gave him a light kiss. As soon as their lips met, a hunger flashed through both of them. In a moment they were in each other's arms, their mouths grinding together, touching and tasting, tongues tangled, his hands buried in her hair, her arms circling his neck.

After a few minutes, Rafe groaned and pulled himself away from her.

"Sorry," he said. "I just...wow."

She said, "You don't have to apologize. I kissed you first."

He blinked. "Oh," he said. "That's right, you did."

She said, "If I'm going to protect you, I better show you where the rest of the traps are. Because it would be really embarrassing if you hurt yourself on one of them. How would I explain to your alpha?"

Which was a reminder that he was going to have to convince her to talk to Jace. Because if he didn't hear from Rafe, he would be coming over here whether either of them liked it or not. But he didn't want to say anything right now. Things were going well. Sort of. Unless Terin shoved him into one of her traps.

He followed her around the property. The thin cotton skirt billowed around her legs, showing tantalizing glimpses of them as it moved and clung. He was very aware of the fact that she hadn't put on any underwear, and he couldn't shake the fantasy of sliding his hands under the flowing cloth to stroke her silky core, or bunching the skirt around her waist and feeling her ride his erection.

He almost slapped himself on the side of the head to stop the images from coming. He wanted her so fiercely—wanted to ride her hard, to hold her close and worship her body. He wanted to sit on the porch swing with her and hold hands and listen to her tell him everything she was thinking. And tell her everything he'd never told anyone else. And then he wanted to fuck her like she was a goddess.

They did a tour of the traps, and Rafe made mental notes about where they all were. They covered the perimeter in such a way that they were pretty decent protection. But they weren't an adequate defense against men with assault weapons.

When he brought that up, Terin took him into the house. She lifted up a loose floorboard at the side of the living room, under a rug, and Rafe whistled.

The space underneath was full of weapons. Rifles, handguns, a couple of assault rifles and a freakin' machine gun. There was even... "Is that a grenade launcher?" he asked, stunned.

"Yeah," she said. "I told you Ben was paranoid."

And Ben had friends in military places, clearly. That made Rafe think.

"Do you think these hunters could be friends of Ben's?" he said. "They seemed like military or paramilitary types. Their weapons weren't just hunting weapons."

Terin looked down, carefully moving a box of ammo into precise alignment with the others.

"Maybe," she said. "He didn't really talk about his background. But he had to know people like that. I mean, he got these from somewhere, didn't he? They don't exactly sell them in Wal-Mart."

"Exactly," Rafe said. "Kane and Israel are down in town now trying to find out more about these guys, where they come from, how long they've been around. They should have answers in a day or two."

She sat back on her heels. "Your pack is doing that? Why? These people are after me, not them."

Rafe hesitated before he answered, choosing his words, which was not usual for him. Usually he just blurted out whatever he was thinking, to the detriment of all concerned.

"Two reasons," he said finally. "One, is because they're good people. They're not going to let another shifter get hunted without trying to do something about it. And they know I'm worried about you, despite your obvious ability to take care of yourself."

She smiled her faint smile at that. Rafe was beginning to realize that was Terin's version of an ear-to-ear grin.

"And, to be honest, the other reason was more self-serving. We need to find out if these men are a threat to the pack as well. We're pretty well protected on our territory; Jace, as a mated alpha, can draw on the land itself to shore up our defenses. But we can't stay inside our territory all the time, and the boundary magic isn't infallible. It helps, especially against humans accidentally wandering onto our land, but it won't keep out a group of determined enemies who know what we are. These guys could attack us if they really wanted to."

She turned away from him, her hair falling over her

face like a curtain.

He wondered if she knew more about the men than she was telling.

"Terin? Do you have any idea who these men might be, or why they're here? Maybe something Ben said?"

She shook her head. "Ben's been gone now for…four years," she said. "If they were friends of his, why would they only be coming now? It doesn't make sense."

It didn't. It would make more sense if they were Alexander Grant's men, coming after Emma. But then why were they specifically looking for a white wolf? None of this fit together. Unless…

"What about from before that?"

She kept her head turned away. "What do you mean?"

She knew what he meant, though. He could feel her body tense. He hated to bring this up, but he had to. "What if the 'accident' that took your memory wasn't an accident? What if someone was trying to hurt you? What if they're still trying?"

"That's crazy. It was ten years ago. How would they have found me after all this time, if they didn't before?" She took a ragged breath. "And anyway, I can't remember. I've tried and tried for years, and it's like pounding on an invisible wall." She knocked on her skull. "There's nothing in here that can help you. Just let it go. I am."

But he could see her hand shaking. Shit. He was upsetting her.

Rafe deliberately turned his attention back to the

arsenal.

"So, do you know how to use any of this?" Rafe had trained on a number of different weapons, but he had never fired half this stuff.

She gave him a sideways look. "Of course. Ben taught me. In case the government ever—you know. Invaded."

He tried to imagine quiet Terin shooting an assault rifle, and his mind boggled. Although the idea seemed to be calming her down.

"I'm glad you like me," he said. "I have a feeling you're lethal, if you don't."

She said softly, almost too quietly for him to hear, "Sometimes I'm lethal even if I do like you."

Rafe didn't know what to say to that.

He spent the day with Terin, helping her restack the wood pile and bring in a block of ice from the ice house. He also managed to put away most of the blueberry pie she'd made that morning, which she would not admit she'd baked for him. He hoped she had, though. It would mean she had been hoping he'd come back.

He thought of calling Jace a few times, but each time he put it off. Things were going so well, and he didn't want to freak Terin out.

When it started to get dark, he tried to help her make dinner, which was less of a disaster than it could have been. But not by much.

"You really don't have any useful skills, do you," she teased, when he'd made a mess of the carrots she'd asked him to chop. "Besides fighting and entertainment, I mean."

"Yes I do," he protested, laughing. "I can lumberjack the hell out of a mountainside. And I can build a cabin and fix a truck, too."

"But I'm pretty sure you can't cook."

"Nope," he admitted. "That's why I really came back," he added. "So you'd make me food."

She turned away, but he could see her smiling to herself in the way he loved. Rafe knew at that moment he was a goner. He'd do anything to see that smile.

After dinner, they sat outside on the porch swing, watching the sunset.

"Have you done any other jobs?" she asked. "Besides the sexy lumberjack thing?"

She thought he was sexy? Hell yeah.

He tried to keep his excitement to himself. "Oh, yeah. I was a long-haul truck driver, for a while, and I worked on oil rigs in Alaska—anything that paid a lot and didn't have to be done inside." He hated being cooped up. "We all did it—me and Jace and Kane and Israel. We had to, so we could get money to buy the land for the pack. That was all we wanted, from the time that our other pack was scattered."

Terin took his hand. "How old were you?" she asked.

Rafe said, "Fifteen." The old sadness welled up in his chest, and Terin tightened her hand around his, as if she could feel it.

"What happened?" she asked.

Rafe usually didn't talk about this. As in, he never talked about it. But she was going to be his mate. He hoped. He wanted her to know.

"There was a rival pack who wanted our territory," he said. "It was beautiful land, in the mountains of Montana. Our pack had been there for generations. Anyway, our pack alpha, Jace's father, hadn't taken a true mate."

At Terin's questioning look, he said, "Some wolves—shifters—have a connection with a special person. You're fated to be together. Soulmates. It's a very intense bond, and not everybody finds it." He stopped, thinking about it. "Probably not everybody even wants it, because it's more than love. You're bound together, forever."

"It sounds kind of nice," Terin said.

"Yeah," Rafe said. That was an understatement, to judge from Jace and Emma. They were the sun in each other's sky. And Rafe was beginning to understand how that felt—and how agonizing it was when you didn't know if the other person wanted it.

"It's something you have to have if you're establishing a pack in a new territory, like we were. The alpha has to find his fated mate and bond with her, to create the magic that binds the pack together and to the territory, like Jace did with Emma. But in an established territory, alphas don't always do that. And Jace's dad didn't. He was crazy in love with Jace's mom, but she...well, she thought she'd found her true mate after she'd mated with Jace's dad. He was in the rival pack."

"Oh, no," Terin murmured. "Was that why they attacked?"

"Kind of," Rafe said. "Not to seize Jace's mom. Her mate's alpha used her to breach our defenses and invade our territory. We had no warning—didn't know what hit us. And Jace's dad waited too long to activate the boundary magic because his mate was on the other side."

"What happened then?" Terin asked. He knew she already knew, but she was giving him the chance to tell her, to unburden himself. He'd never actually told the story before; everyone he was close enough to had been there, and nobody wanted to talk about it.

Rafe felt like he was traveling deep inside the hidden parts of himself. "They killed most of our pack," he said. "I'll never forget it. Fights going on everywhere, through the woods, blood and heat and howling. And bodies." He heard his voice shaking. "Bodies everywhere, of people I loved."

Terin slid her arm through his and leaned her head on his shoulder. Her presence shored him up, spread a balm over the raw and ragged edges of his heart.

"I tried to fight," he said. "But I was young, and so scared I was shaking, and the first one almost took me apart. The last thing I remember was being thrown against a tree and hitting my head, hard. I think they left me for dead."

He thought about the other night. "That seems to happen to me a lot," he added. He was trying for smartass, but it came out kind of shaky.

Terin smiled and began stroking his arm gently. The shakiness started to subside.

"I didn't help at all," he said. "All my life, everybody said what a fighter I was. It was all I was really good at. I was training to be an Enforcer. But when the worst went down, I folded like a bad hand of poker." It was his deepest shame, one he'd never confided to anyone.

Terin didn't say anything, didn't try to fix his feelings or talk him out of them. She just kept leaning against him and gently stroking his arm, and he felt comfort and caring pouring into him like clear water, filling him up.

Rafe gave a great sigh, feeling like some of the burden he'd been carrying had been lifted off him.

"When I woke up, I found out that Jace had protected me while I was unconscious. Me and Jesse. He'd fought off three of the invaders, and then shifted and carried me to safety."

He took a shaky breath. "For a long time, we thought we were all that was left. Gradually, we heard about a few of the pack who had scattered, gone in different directions, and were hiding out. But they had no territory, no home. So we had to build them one."

She said, "And you did it. Against all the odds, you got your territory. You rebuilt your pack."

Rafe nodded. "Yeah. We were so happy, you know?" He hesitated, not sure how to say what he was feeling. "But Jesse was the one who put us over the top.

He turned out to be some kind of computer genius, and he wrote some apps that made a shit ton of money. He's totally the brains of the operation. And Jace is a natural alpha. Every wolf in the pack would do damn near anything for him. And now he has Emma…"

And he doesn't need me. Nobody needs me.

But he couldn't say that out loud. He'd just sound like a whiny drama queen, wanting to be the first and the best.

"But you were a big part of it," Terin said. "You all did it together."

"Yeah," Rafe said. But he wasn't convinced, and he could tell she knew it. But she had sense enough to leave it alone, and change the subject instead.

"This Emma," Terin said. "She's human? Not a shifter?"

Rafe shook his head. "Nope. We didn't even think it was possible, that a human could be a shifter's fated mate. But it happened. Emma and Jace bonded, and it was like…I can't describe it. Every wolf in the pack was aware of every other wolf, all at the same time. We could *feel* each other, and feel Jace's presence. And when he bonded with the territory—it was like all the energy from the trees and rocks and the mountain was pouring through him into us, so that we were a part of it, and it was a part of us."

He grinned ruefully. "I suck at describing things."

"No you don't," she said. "I understood what you meant. I even feel that sometimes, a little bit. With this land."

"Really?" he asked, surprised. "I wonder if a lone wolf can bond with their territory. Without a mate." He hoped it wasn't true. If she was bonded here, she'd never leave. He couldn't stand that thought.

She shrugged. "I don't know. If I ever knew any of this, about how things work with shifters, I don't remember it," she said.

She added, "So your mission, what you all set out to do, is complete." Rafe nodded. Then she surprised him. "So why is there still a hole inside you?"

To cover his confusion, he countered, "What makes you think there is?"

She simply said, "I can feel it."

That made his whole inside go still. She could feel what he felt? Was she feeling the mating bond? He was afraid to ask.

"I don't know," he said, in answer to her question. "It's been bugging me ever since Jace and Emma bonded. I mean, I'm supposed to be ecstatic, right? We have our pack. I'm the Second. We got everything we ever wanted. And yet…"

"You're not happy," she said. She kissed his shoulder, and then laid her cheek against it again.

"I feel like an ungrateful jerk," Rafe admitted. "I don't know what I want."

"Maybe you need another mission," Terin said.

Rafe put his arm around her and pulled her close. Maybe he did.

CHAPTER 12

They sat there for a while, watching the sunset, sipping beer from the icebox. Gradually, Terin felt the restlessness in Rafe settle, and he began to relax. He had slipped his arm around her and was holding her against him, his cheek resting on her hair. She loved feeling the warmth of him, the solidness, the strength.

All too soon, though, she felt like she couldn't hold her eyes open any longer.

"I need some sleep," she said. "I didn't get much last night."

He ruffled her hair. "Missing me?" he said.

"Yes," she said, before she could stop herself.

He pulled slightly away and turned to look in her eyes. "Were you?" he asked. His voice sounded casual, but she could see hope in his eyes. Like he'd really wanted her to say yes.

After the raw honesty of his confessions earlier, that light of hope broke something in her heart. Instead of answering, she pulled his mouth to hers. As soon as their lips touched, the now-familiar desire rose up inside her. This feeling that if only she could get close enough to him, unlock her soul, then the hole within him would be filled.

He rose to his feet and pulled her against him, the full length of their bodies pressed together. She wound her arms around his neck, trying to pull him even closer. She suddenly didn't want to let him go. She wanted to wrap herself around him, to ease that hurt, fill the emptiness in him that even creating a new pack hadn't assuaged.

He growled low in his throat, the sound sending a rush of heat pooling between her legs. His lips moved across her cheek and down the side of her neck, nipping, biting, soothing, kissing.

She could feel his cock against her, straining against his jeans, only that and the thin layer of her skirt between them. She wanted to pull off all her clothes and be naked with him under the stars, but the thought of the men in the woods made her think again.

She broke away and took his hands, pulling him inside.

"Bar the door," she said, her voice husky. He did what she asked, and then she led him into the bedroom. Once there, she pulled him toward her once again.

He said, "You don't have to do this. You know. Just because I'm protecting you."

"You forgot," she whispered in his ear. "I'm protecting you. So I need to keep you close."

He gave a ragged laugh. She could hear him struggling to control his breathing, and was amazed that she could do that to him.

He said, "That's good. Because all day, I haven't

been able to stop thinking about you being naked under that skirt."

She nipped his ear and said, "I'm always naked under my clothes. Aren't you?"

He groaned. "I don't suppose you want to see?"

She nodded, feeling suddenly bold. "Uh huh."

He froze, as if he was hoping he'd heard right. She slid her hands under the hem of his t-shirt. She lifted, and he ducked his head and slid his arms out.

The magnificence of his muscled chest still took her breath away. She ran her fingertips lightly over the place where the sharp branch had impaled him. The wound was healed, although the scar was still red and angry. She kissed the place where he had been hurt, and then ran her tongue around it. She felt him shiver.

His reaction made her bolder. She kissed her way across his chest to his flat nipples, and licked them until they stood up. He growled, his chest rumbling. She ran her hands across his chest and around to his back, and then began kissing up his neck. He bent his head so she could reach, and she bit him lightly under the ear. He growled again, a deep sound of pleasure.

"I want to run my hands under that skirt and stroke you," he murmured. "Your thighs, your ass, your pussy—all of you."

She could feel her animal nature rising. She loved that feeling—loved the feeling of Rafe's wolf rising to meet her. Ben had never stirred this part of her, never ignited the animal fire inside her. For the first time, she loved her wolf.

Rafe made her feel whole.

"Take me," she whispered. "Touch me. Light me on fire."

Rafe growled again, and then slid her skirt up and wrapped his arms around her butt, lifting her so her legs straddled his hips. She slipped her arms around his neck and kissed him, deep, tasting him and stroking him with her tongue. She wanted to taste all of him, to lose herself in the feel of his skin, his scent, the feeling of him thrusting inside her.

He pulled her against him, and she could feel his bulge pressed against the delicate, sensitive skin of her pussy. She moaned and tangled her fingers in his hair, rolling her hips against him.

Rafe carried her the few steps over to the bed and laid her down. He reached for the zipper of his jeans, but she pushed his hands away and unzipped them herself. She'd seen his cock before, but not like it was now, full and hard. She pushed down his jeans—he wasn't wearing underwear either.

"Look who's talking about being naked under your clothes," she said wickedly.

He grinned. "If I'd told you before, would you have been thinking all day about me being naked?" he asked.

"I already was," she confessed.

His grin got wider, and then faded with a gasp as she wrapped her hand around his cock and stroked it.

She leaned forward impulsively and tasted it, something she'd never done with Ben. She loved the way Rafe tasted, the way he gasped and tangled his fingers in her hair when he felt her mouth on him.

She licked slowly, running her tongue over the head of his cock, and he groaned.

"Oh, babe. That's—" He couldn't even finish his sentence.

She licked and sucked until Rafe pulled away with a groan and slid her tank top up over her head. She saw the look in his eyes when he saw her breasts, the tenderness with which he touched them. He pushed her back on the bed and took them in his mouth, sucking erotically first on one nipple, and then the other—licking, sucking, tugging gently. Wet heat rushed into her pussy, and she almost came right then. Then he slid his hand up her thigh, pushing up her skirt, and stroked her slick, silky folds.

Terin thought she was going to die. She put her head back and moaned, losing herself in the sensations. She could feel Rafe getting hotter and hotter, as if she could sense what he was feeling somehow. She wanted to make him feel the way she felt.

"Rafe," she murmured. "I want you now."

He closed his eyes for a second, and then said, "Not yet."

He kissed his way down to her stomach, and then pulled her skirt off her hips and moved between her legs. He began trailing his lips down her thigh, alternately kissing and nipping the tender skin.

Just as he got near her pussy, he switched to the other leg, starting down by the knee and kissing his way up again. She was already bunching the covers in her hands, wanting him to taste her, but not knowing how to ask. Ben had never done this.

When Rafe's tongue finally slicked between the folds of her pussy, she thought she would explode. She moaned and writhed, wanting him to kiss and lick every part of her. He flicked his tongue over her clit, then swirled and sucked it. He moved down to thrust his tongue inside her, and then licked her slowly, in broad, fat strokes, until Terin saw stars.

Her orgasm crashed over her, making her tremble and cry out under the waves and waves of sensation. Just as it was beginning to ebb, Rafe moved up and slid his cock into her in one smooth, hard thrust.

She almost came again, right then.

He pulled back and then thrust slowly into her again, letting her adjust to accommodate him, drawing him inside her and settling him between her hips.

He kissed her, and the taste of herself on his lips was incredibly erotic, salty and sweet. He cupped her head in his hands and looked into her eyes.

"Okay?" he asked.

She just nodded, unable to speak. He smiled and began to move, first slowly, and then harder and faster as she moved her hips to meet his. She felt her orgasm spiraling up again, and she grabbed the firm muscles of his ass, raising her hips to pull him all the way inside her. Rafe thrust into her, losing himself, digging his fingers into her hair and saying her name.

"God, Terin, you're so beautiful. So amazing. Tell me you're mine. I need you…"

"I'm yours," she whispered. "I want all of you. Take me."

And the words felt right. For once she didn't think of the future, only this feeling right now, the feeling that they belonged together, were part of each other. "You're mine," she said.

With a final thrust, he came inside her, and she felt a sudden rush she couldn't explain. Like his soul had exploded into hers and she could feel everything that he felt, feel everything outside the cabin and inside it, as if it were all alive and she could see it all. The feeling spiraled out, out, and then back in, until nothing existed but the two of them, as if they were sharing the same skin.

CHAPTER 13

A long time later, Rafe woke up in the dark, aware that he felt cold and alone. The bed next to him was empty; Terin was gone. And she'd been gone awhile, to judge by what little warmth was left where she'd been lying.

Worry stabbed through him. Where was she?

Rafe got up and padded through the house, even checking her painting studio. She wasn't anywhere. There were no lights burning, but his wolf eyes could see in the dark, and there was moonlight. He could find his way.

He pulled on his jeans and walked out onto the porch, sniffing the air. He couldn't scent Terin nearby. Where the hell had she gone? And why had she gone alone? What was the point of having him here to protect her if she went wandering off on her own whenever the mood took her?

He walked around the yard, trying to pick up the freshest scent, but there were too many competing trails. Finally, he went into the kitchen and pulled a beer out of the icebox. He sat down with it on the porch swing and swung back and forth, back and forth, watching the stars, and waiting for his mate to return.

After a long time, he sensed her. He'd attuned himself to the night, to the land. To her. He could feel her when she came near.

He tried to keep his emotions within himself, trying not to be impatient, not to spook her in case she could feel him the way he felt her. His lovely, mysterious mate had given herself to him, but she still had too many secrets, too little trust.

She ghosted out of the forest like the spirit wolf she resembled, standing right at the edge, looking at him without moving. He just sat and looked back at her.

This was a woman who could not be forced, could not be convinced. She was wild, wilder even than he was, and she would only come to him when she felt safe.

So he sat and waited. It was the hardest thing he'd ever done.

After a long time, she walked over behind the shed. When she came out she'd shifted back to human form, and had a loose dress on. He still didn't say anything, just sat there, trying not to seem tense or upset, just keeping himself open to her so that she would want to come and sit by him.

After a moment's hesitation, she sat down next to him on the porch swing. He slid his hand tentatively over and wrapped his fingers around hers.

"Everything okay?" he asked.

She nodded. He waited, his natural impatience making him crazy, but trying to keep his breathing even and his touch easy.

After a long silence, she added, "I couldn't stay

inside."

He nodded. "You could have woken me up. I wouldn't have minded."

She shrugged. "I needed to be alone."

He let out a long breath. There was no point in asking her why—it was just the way she was. It was what she was used to.

But it killed him to think she needed to get away from him, when all he wanted was to be near her.

"Do you wish you were still alone?" he asked finally. "Right now?"

She didn't answer.

He tried not to show his emotion, but he couldn't help letting his shoulders slump in disappointment.

"You do, don't you. You wish I wasn't here."

"It's not—" she broke off, clearly frustrated because she didn't know how to explain herself. So he waited some more.

"It's not you," she said. "Or—not exactly. When we were together, I felt—"

She paused again, then went on, "I've never felt like that. I wanted to be inside you and share your skin. I felt like we were one person, and—"

His impulsiveness took over, and he couldn't stop himself from finishing her sentence.

"It scared you," he said softly.

She nodded.

"It scares me too," he admitted. "But—I want to open up to you. Why don't you want to open up to me?"

He was trying his damnedest not to sound plaintive.

Pathetic. But he probably did.

"I do," she said. "And—I don't. It's too hard when the person isn't there anymore, or when they change their mind about you."

He wanted to say he wouldn't do that, but he sensed that wasn't what she wanted or needed to hear. It was too easy to say, and too easy to think of all the ways that promise might not be able to be kept.

Instead, he asked, "What happened with your husband?"

She stayed silent so long, he thought she wasn't going to answer.

Finally she said, "He didn't know I was a shifter. He found me when I was sixteen, like I told you, and I didn't remember anything about myself. I knew I could change to wolf, but I sensed it was dangerous for me if he knew, because he wasn't like me. I knew there were others like me, but I didn't know where they were or how I knew. And there were no other shifter wolves around here then."

Rafe nodded, stroking her fingers gently with his.

She went on, "So I hid it from him. I used to go out in the woods a lot on my own. I'd look for herbs and plants, and just walk. Ben just thought I liked to hike, and that I needed to go off by myself sometimes. He didn't mind that. He lived out here because he was a recluse, so we both needed to be alone sometimes. And he had his projects—his traps and his weapons, and his conspiracy theories."

Rafe snorted. He still didn't understand any of that,

110

how someone could be so wacked out.

"So," she went on, "I'd go off by myself, and when I was far from the house I'd shift. I got in the habit of keeping stuff stashed in different caves, in case I needed to shift back when I was away from home. I'd even go out at night sometimes, and run and run, up the mountain to this cliff where I could look out over the whole valley. And I'd watch the stars, and the sunsets, and I'd come back and paint what life looked like from the other side of me. From my secret self."

Rafe said quietly, "So what went wrong?"

She sighed. "He started to get suspicious. He'd always been paranoid about other people, about the government, but never about me. But he got worse and worse—I think he was really mentally ill, you know? And so he started wanting to know where I went, who I saw, accusing me of informing on him to all kinds of people. Then he started saying things about demons and Judgment Day. For a while I stayed close to the cabin, but then I couldn't stand it anymore. I felt like I couldn't breathe, and my wolf was clawing its way out, and I had to do something. So I'd sneak out when he was asleep."

Rafe could see where this was probably going, but he said nothing, just squeezed her hand encouragingly.

"He'd been building all these traps," she said. "That's when he started with that, and stockpiled the weapons. Anyway, one night I went out and shifted, and he followed me. I wasn't paying attention—it never occurred to me that he would spy on me. He waited for me at the cave where I left my clothes, and he saw me shift back from wolf to human."

Rafe winced. "He freaked out, I imagine."

She nodded. "But way worse than I thought he would. He started going on about monsters and demons, and he shot at me with his rifle. So I ran. I ran so far, farther than I'd ever gone before, and I stayed out for two days. But I had nowhere to go, and I couldn't live as a wolf forever, any more than I could live as a human without shifting. So eventually I went back to the cabin.

"Ben was walking through the woods, without his gun, calling me. Saying he was sorry, begging me to come back, if I could hear him. To come home."

She shifted her weight uncomfortably. Rafe stroked the back of her hand with his thumb. "It's okay," he whispered.

She nodded. "I watched the cabin for another day. He spent most of his time looking for me, trying to get me to come back. So finally I did."

"What happened?" Rafe asked. He knew it couldn't have been good.

She said bitterly, "He shot me with a tranquilizer gun. He said I was a monster. A demon. And he was going to give me to someone who knew how to get rid of the demon. He'd called this man, this demon exorcist. And he was coming."

Rafe whistled. "Someone who was going to take away your ability to shift?"

She shook her head. "I don't think so," she said. "I mean, that's what Ben thought, but I think he was really crazy by then. Because the man came, a few days later, and it was nothing like that. Ben had put me in a cage in the shed…"

She broke off, her voice shaking. It was all Rafe could do not to punch something. That her husband—the man she trusted to take care of her—had locked her up like a zoo animal made him want to stand up and break things. Instead, he wrapped both arms gently around her.

"Oh, sweetheart," he said. "I'm so sorry."

She took a long, shuddering breath. Rafe knew she needed the catharsis, just like he'd needed it earlier. But he hadn't realized how painful it was to listen to the heartbreak of someone you loved and relive it with them.

Terin got her voice back. "The man was dressed like the ones you told me about—in camouflage hunting clothes. Not like a priest or anything. And when he saw me, he called me 'an excellent specimen.' Like I was some kind of collector's item. And when he found out I was a white wolf, he got all excited." Her voice got very dry. "Apparently, I'm rare and exotic."

"Actually, you are," Rafe said. "I've never seen another white wolf shifter. Or heard of one, for that matter."

"Yep, that's me, one of a kind," she said bitterly.

Rafe said quietly, "You're the most beautiful wolf I've ever seen. And the most beautiful woman."

He felt her soften beside him, and he could see tears brimming in her eyes, but they didn't fall. He wondered how many times in her life she'd had to hold back tears. He moved closer to her.

After a deep shaky breath, she continued her story.

"So, this man didn't seem to have any interest in demons or monsters. It was more like—he was buying a show dog, or something. He was going to take me away somewhere. I don't know what he wanted with me, but I got the feeling he didn't want me for himself. It wasn't that kind of interest—you know, greedy and acquisitive. It was more like he was trying to figure out how much I was worth to other people."

"You think this guy was going to sell you?" Rafe was shocked to his core.

She frowned. "That doesn't happen?" she asked. "For some reason I thought it did. Not a lot, but sometimes. By a few humans that knew about us."

Rafe drew his eyebrows together, searching his memory.

"Not that I know of," he said. "I mean, we told stories, when we were kids, but it was more like boogeyman stories, you know? About how someone was going to come and snatch you up to sell you to a collector, or to a group that wanted to let you loose so they could hunt you down. Or stuff you and put you on their mantelpiece."

She winced. He kissed the top of her head in apology.

He said, "But it those were just stories we told each other around the campfire. Our pack does some Enforcer contract work, dealing with problems between packs, or rogue shifters, but I don't know of any documented cases of shifters being taken by humans. But then, so many species don't have any kind of central organization, so isolated cases may never get reported."

That was disturbing.

She said, "I don't know. It's like the other knowledge that I have from before—knowing things but not knowing where I learned them, or how. So I can't tell if that belief is factual, or just an impression I had, or stories I heard as a kid, like you did."

Rafe made a mental note to mention that to Jace and Kane. They could find out if the Council knew anything about trafficking in shifters. The mere thought made him feel sick.

"Anyway," Rafe said, "What happened with this man?"

Terin's gaze grew faraway, like she was seeing into the past. "Ben didn't realize about shifter metabolism and healing," she said. "He'd shot me full of tranquilizers, but they were for humans, and he gave me a human dose. It wore off before he thought it would, even though he reassured the man that he'd doped me up good. And I pretended to be groggier than I was, so he'd think I was weak."

Rafe said, "So you fought?" Good for her.

She nodded. "When they were taking me out of the cage for transport. I shifted and fought them both, and tried to run," she said.

"The man tried to kill me then, but I wounded him. Ben ran after me when I tried to escape. He'd been building traps while I was gone—new ones. I didn't know where they all were. So when I was running for the woods, I barely avoided one of them. He was so agitated that he went right into one of the pit traps."

She bit her lip.

"I couldn't save him," she said sadly, tears running down her cheeks. "He was impaled on the stakes, and he died. And that man—he was still coming. I remember him standing at the edge of the pit, towering over me. I'd turned human again so I could try to help Ben. And he just looked down at me over the barrel of his gun with this horrible grin on his face, and I picked up Ben's gun and I shot him. Dead."

She was trembling. "It's okay," said Rafe, stroking her hair. "It's okay. You're okay."

She started to cry for real, then. He continued to hold her, gentling her, letting her get it out. She'd lived with this all alone ever since that day. He realized she must have gotten rid of the man's body somewhere in the woods, on her own, and then buried Ben at the edge of the forest where his grave still stood.

"I can't imagine what that must have been like for you," he whispered. "I'm sorry you had to go through it all alone."

She struggled to get herself together; he could feel her pushing her emotions back down. "I've always been alone," she said. "Even when I was with Ben, in a way I was still alone. He didn't really know me."

Rafe nodded. He wanted to say that he knew her, that he thought she was strong and beautiful inside and out. But he knew that she couldn't believe him, not right now. Words were easy. The only thing she would trust were his actions, day after day after day. Loyalty and understanding took time.

She said, "I never loved Ben, even though I cared about him. And I don't know if he ever really loved me. But he was kind to me. He rescued me, and he treated me well until...until he couldn't."

Until he lost his mind. She must have been so scared.

She pulled back and looked at Rafe.

"So now you know what I'm like," she said. "I like you, Rafe. I really do." She sighed. "But you need...so much more. You deserve so much more. You're kind and gentle and loving, and you need a woman who appreciates that. Who wants to be in your pack with you, and have cubs, and all that. Who can help *you* be part of the pack."

"I want you," he said. He couldn't stop himself. "I want you and your paintings and your past and your walks in the woods alone. I just want to make you happy."

"But don't you see?" she said. "I've never been happy. I don't know if I ever can be happy. There's something broken inside me that you can't fix. All I'd do is make you feel like you were never enough, that you could never do enough. That's not fair. You'd end up miserable, with the same hole in your heart you have now. Only bigger, because I would have torn out the part where the hope was."

Rafe just pulled her close again. She resisted for a minute, but then she nestled into him. He just wanted to protect her from the whole world. To keep her safe always, to love her and watch her blossom under his love. But he couldn't force it.

"Maybe you're right," he said. "But I wish you'd give me the chance. Give *us* the chance. To just see if we could be happy together."

She sighed, and he said, nudging her gently, "It could happen."

"In your dreams," she said, but he could feel her smiling. And right then, it was enough.

CHAPTER 14

Terin led Rafe back inside. She was so tired, after telling him her story. She didn't know exactly why she'd told him. She'd never told anyone—but then, she'd never had anyone to tell. Except for a few shopkeepers in town, she hadn't talked to anyone since Ben died.

And they hadn't talked much, either. Ben wasn't one for long conversations. They would go for days in companionable silence, barely saying a word to each other.

Rafe liked to talk, and he liked to listen. It was strange.

They went back to bed, and she snuggled up beside him. He made love to her again—this time slow and sweet, gentle and loving. She felt like he touched every part of her, inside and out. That he found every raw and ragged place and tried to gentle it.

But she was too raw. She'd been hurt too badly.

Just the same, it soothed her some. He looked into her eyes, opened his heart to her, showed her with every touch and kiss the way he felt about her. It warmed her from the inside out, and yet at the same time it broke her heart. He had so much to give, and she would only hurt him. She would hurt him if she mated with him, and she would hurt him if she didn't.

But for this one night, she laced her fingers through his, looked into his eyes, and let him love her. Just for this one night.

The next morning, Terin was up at dawn as usual. Lots needed doing in the garden, and she liked doing it in the cool of the morning, before the sun got too hot.

Feeing mischievous, she dragged Rafe out of bed as well.

"What the hell?" he complained. "It's the middle of the night."

She poked him. "Is not. It's morning. Don't you hear the birds?"

"Stupid birds," she heard him mutter. "I eat birds. I don't listen to them." He pulled the pillow over his head.

"Oh, no," she said. "You tell me you want to be with me, and then you expect me to do all the work? I don't think so."

Her tone was teasing, but she really wanted to see what he was made of. Was he willing to work? To be a partner? Or was he the feckless drifter he claimed to be?

She put him to work chopping firewood, pausing to admire the play of his muscles as he worked shirtless. She saw the smug look on his face when he caught her watching, and shook her head at him. He just grinned.

She was working in the garden with her hoe, chopping the weeds that seemed to grow overnight, when suddenly she felt a stream of water soak the back of her shirt.

She swung around. Rafe was standing at the edge of the garden, a huge plastic water gun in his hands.

"What the hell is that?" she demanded.

He smirked at her.

"It's a Supersoaker," he said. "It has come to my attention that you're suffering from a serious deficit of fun. It's my job to rectify that. Prepare for battle."

He squirted her again.

She rose to her feet. "No fair," she objected. "I don't have a weapon."

"I brought two," he said.

He reached down at his feet and picked up an identical gun off the ground. He tossed it to her. It was heavy—he'd already filled it with water.

"So you just happened to have a couple of giant water guns in the back of your truck," she said.

He looked at her innocently. "Doesn't everybody?"

She shook her head. Then, without warning, she raised the gun and shot him right in the face. Spluttering, he said, "Hey! We were in a cease-fire!"

"Sucker!" she said, dashing out of the garden and ducking around the corner of the house.

The battle raged throughout the yard. They stalked each other, taking cover behind trees and outbuildings. After an hour, both of them were soaked, but there was no clear winner.

Finally, Terin sneaked up behind Rafe and pushed him into a mud puddle. He slipped and went down with a splash.

Terin started laughing hysterically at the sight of him covered in mud. She went to help him up, and he pulled her down in the mud on top of him.

"Hey!" she said. "You're getting me dirty!"

He pinned her to the ground. "I like you dirty," he said, giving her a huge leer.

"Pervert," she said.

"Uh huh," he agreed. He kissed her, his hands roaming up to her soaked shirt. "You should really get out of these wet clothes," he murmured.

"So should you," she said. "But if you think I'm having sex with you in the middle of a hog wallow, think again. And anyway, I won the fight. I get to be in charge."

"Who says you won?" Rafe said.

"I did," she informed him. "My sneak attack disabled you. I captured you, and now you're my prisoner. You have to do whatever I say."

"Really?" Rafe looked hopeful. "Are you going to make me do dirty sexual things? Because if you are, then I totally concede the battle."

Terin stood and picked up the water gun, and pointed it at him.

"Stand up," she said. He complied, grinning.

She looked him up and down, and saw his eyes begin to flash with hot gold. "Take your pants off," she said.

He did it slowly, tantalizing her. His cock was already standing up, and she could feel heat pooling between her legs.

"March to the shed," she said. He obeyed her, marching across the yard to the small wooden structure. His ass was gorgeous, the muscles flexing as he walked. She shot him once in it with the water gun, just to see him jump. He growled, but she could tell he was enjoying this.

When they got inside, she made him spread a blanket on the pile of hay in the corner. Then she stood in the middle of it, dropped the gun, peeled off her sundress and commanded, "Kneel."

Rafe's eyes flashed gold. He knelt in front of her, his hands sliding up the back of her thighs, caressing her.

Terin's wolf growled in pleasure. Seeing his muscled, naked body at her feet was incredibly arousing. "Kiss me," she demanded boldly.

She felt his warm breath on the soft curls around her pussy. His lips moved against her mound in slow, deep kisses, his tongue sliding into her slit. He kissed her clit as if he were kissing her mouth, tasting, sucking, delving deep and then pulling back with gentle sips before kissing her hard once more.

Terin gave a low whimper, her knees buckling. Rafe supported her easily, his hands cupping her ass, holding her against him as she wrapped her fingers in his hair and held on. It was hot, wild and glorious. It was too much, but he pulled her closer, not letting her escape his relentless lips and tongue, making her writhe against him and beg for release.

Just as she was losing control, he sat back and pulled

her down onto his lap, right onto his swollen cock. He rubbed it between her pussy lips, tantalizing her.

"Take me," she begged. "Please, Rafe."

He locked his hot gaze onto hers, then drew her toward him, his lips against her mouth. "Who's in charge now?" he murmured.

He caught her lower lip between his teeth and bit gently, then kissed her long and deep. Terin rocked her hips against him, rubbing along his cock, moaning.

He shifted her weight and thrust himself inside her, filling her. The moment the base of his cock touched her clit she exploded around him, shaking with every thrust, reveling in the hunger in his golden eyes. He laid her down and pulled her legs up so that he could thrust deep into her, and she urged him on with mindless whimpers. She couldn't get enough of him.

He thrust more deeply still, until he tensed and hot warmth shot into her, filling her. Slowly, the tempest calmed, and they clung to each other, trembling.

They lay together, their ragged breathing slowing and synchronizing, neither of them able to talk. They made love again, teasing each other with their hands, their mouths, touching and retreating until finally Rafe pinned her to the ground once more and claimed every part of her, and sent her spiraling into the stratosphere once again. She couldn't imagine how she had ever lived without this, without even knowing that it existed outside of fiction. Without knowing that someone could make her feel so amazing. So alive.

She had to have all of him. She rolled him on his

back and straddled him, easing herself down on his cock. He stroked her breasts, her hips, as he filled her completely.

She gave a growl, raking her nails lightly over his chest, and she felt his wolf growl in return. Sexy beast.

She moved over him, rocking her hips, raising and lowering herself to sheathe and release him. She tipped her head back, losing herself in the sensations, and she could feel him pushing into her harder as she reveled in the knowledge that he was losing control as well.

As the fire began to spread through her, he reached out and stroked her clit with his thumb, sending her into orbit once more.

He pulled her close then, so that she lay on top of him, his arms around her. He began thrusting harder, faster, and she urged him on until she felt him come, throbbing inside her and calling out her name.

Afterwards she lay on his chest, spent, feeling the aftershocks and the way he relaxed underneath her. He kept running his hands over her back, her butt, her hair, as if he couldn't stop touching her. She just wanted to stay curled up with him forever.

His phone started ringing, outside, and he groaned.

"That's Jace's ringtone," he said. "I have to get it."

"Won't he leave a message?" she asked.

"Yeah. And then he'll drive over here to see why I didn't answer. You know, in case I'm dead or anything."

She moved reluctantly and let him up, feeling suddenly cold and alone. He walked outside, and through the open door she could see him fishing his jeans out of the mud puddle and searching the pockets for his phone. She hoped it was waterproof.

The phone had stopped ringing, but he hit a button and called back. Jace answered right away.

"Yeah," Rafe said hoarsely into the phone. He listened, and then said, "I know. Sorry. It's just—kind of a delicate situation here."

Great, Terin though. She was a 'delicate situation.' Just what every girl wanted to be.

"Um, I'll ask her," Rafe was saying. "Let me call you right back."

He cut off the call and then rubbed the back of his neck. He was obviously uncomfortable.

Terin took pity on him. She got up and went out to him.

"That was him?" she said.

"Yup, that was Jace," he said. Then he added, "My pack alpha."

Terin waited. He knew she knew who Jace was, so she wanted to know why he was explaining again.

Rafe said, "He agreed to let you come and stay with the pack, to protect you from the hunters."

Terin frowned. She'd told him she wasn't leaving.

"If you want," he added hastily, clearly interpreting the look on her face correctly.

"But even if you don't," he went on, "he wants to meet you. You're another wolf, near our territory, and those hunters...we might need to fight them too. He wants to know why they want you."

"I don't know why," she snapped. She didn't like

this. His alpha had no right to come here. "I don't see why he cares about me," she said. "What aren't you telling me?"

Rafe smacked his hand into the mud puddle, sending up a splash of muddy water.

"Shit. Okay," he said. "I told him how I feel about you. And he wants to see if...well, if you and I were mates, you'd be a member of our pack. And he'd be responsible for you. For how you fit in, or if you disrupted the pack dynamics..." he trailed off.

Terin put her fists on her hips. She should have known. This Jace was going to come here and judge her, and decide she wasn't good enough.

"I never asked to be part of your pack," she said. "I don't want to. I told you that."

"I know," Rafe said quietly.

The hurt in his voice made her go still. She absently gathered up her hair, twisting it into a long tail. She hated hurting Rafe. It made the middle of her chest hurt. But she didn't want him going behind her back and arranging things.

He said, "But what if those guys come back? You can't hold out here under an assault like they could bring, no matter how many traps or weapons you have. You're only one person."

She knew that. And it scared her, but Rafe and the pack scared her even more.

"This is my home," she said. "And this Jace doesn't need to come here and see if I'm good enough to be let in your wolf club."

Rafe sighed. "I knew I'd fuck this up," he said. "Would you please just listen?"

She wanted to stalk away. She wanted to shift, and run up the mountain where the air was clear and she didn't have to worry about what anyone thought of her, or what they expected out of her. She could just be herself, the way she was—broken, but free.

But then she looked at Rafe's face. She could feel his emotions, the way she'd been able to feel his feelings since the first night they'd slept together. Before that, even. When they were in the cave, and she was tending his wounds.

She could feel his frustration, his sense of inadequacy that he couldn't convey to her how important this was to him. And she could feel his heart breaking, because his pack was part of him, and she didn't want it. She didn't want him.

She hesitated. The forest was calling her. Freedom was calling her.

Taking a deep breath, she closed her mind to all that and sat down on the ground in front of him.

"Tell me," she said. "Explain what this Jace person wants."

Rafe ran his hands through his hair. "Okay," he said. "I know you don't want to be in a pack. But remember when I told you about true mates?"

She nodded, watching his face. He didn't look at her, just down at the ground in front of him. "Well, regardless of what you feel for me—that's what I feel for you. Ever since the first night I saw you, when I was delirious. I want that forever bond, and I want it with you."

She was stunned. Rafe wanted to bind himself to her forever? To make it permanent and magical, so that she'd know he would always be there?

She didn't know what to say to that. She wanted it desperately, and it terrified her.

"Oh, Rafe," she murmured brokenly.

"I didn't want to pressure you," Rafe said. "But Jace is worried because of the hunters." He looked into her face then, his grin crooked. "And because I'm so messed up over you."

Terin hated to see him hurting. But she didn't know if she could do this. "So if we had this bond thing, I'd have to go live with your pack? There's no other choice?"

Rafe rubbed his hand over his face. "No, there's other choices. But it's complicated."

Which meant he'd have to leave his pack. She couldn't make him do that.

"Look, would you just talk to Jace? Please?" He was almost begging her. Her heart broke a little more.

Terin sighed. "I don't understand why he has to be involved in something that's between us."

"I know," Rafe said. "But I'm involved. And if I'm involved, the pack's involved. That's how it works. And Jace is responsible for the pack. He's my alpha, so if he wants to meet you, you can tell him no, if you want, but I can't."

Terin said, "So you have to do what he says?"

"Well, yeah," Rafe said. "He's the alpha."

"And if I mated with you, I'd have to do what he said too?"

"He's a good guy, Terin," Rafe said. "He wouldn't give you orders just because he felt like it. Only if the good of the pack was involved."

Terin thought about that. "I suppose that wouldn't necessarily be so bad," she said. "I pretty much used to do what Ben said."

Rafe huffed. "So wait. You're telling me you did what Ben said, and you'd do what Jace says. So why the fuck do you never want to do what *I* say?"

"I don't know," Terin said, standing up. "I guess you just bring out the rebel in me." She headed back to the house, but not before she saw him begin to smile.

"I like rebels," he called after her.

"Good thing," she said. Just because she got scared about some things didn't mean she was a pushover.

"Where are you going?"

"To clean up. If I'm going to meet this alpha, I don't want to do it covered in mud."

She heard Rafe mutter something about X chromosomes before he heaved a sigh of relief and started dialing Jace.

CHAPTER 15

Jace and Emma arrived about an hour later. Rafe walked down the road to meet their truck coming in, to talk to them before they met Terin.

"She's a little dubious about the whole pack thing," he said to Jace. "So go easy on her, please? She doesn't ever remember living with a pack, and she's been on her own for a whole lot of years, some of them hiding who she is. She doesn't understand protocol or how she's supposed to act, so don't get mad at her, okay? She seems tough, but she's fragile underneath, and—"

"Relax, Rafe," Jace said. "I'll try not to terrify your princess, okay? I'm really not that scary, and Emma is here to keep me in line."

At Jace's request, Rafe waited outside for him and Emma to speak to Terin alone. Rafe paced up and down the yard, sat down in the swing, and immediately got up again, too restless to sit.

He knew he should have faith in Terin. But Jace and Emma didn't know her. They didn't understand her. And what if she felt like she couldn't talk to them? What if she felt threatened, and shifted and just ran? What if she panicked? What would Jace say then?

It seemed like an eternity until Jace came out of the cabin.

"Where's Emma?" Rafe asked.

"Chill, Rafe," Jace said with a grin. "She and Emma are talking about quilts and preserve recipes."

"Oh," Rafe said, feeling stupid. "I guess it went okay, then?"

Jace's face grew more serious. "She seems nice, Rafe, and she's a lot less unbalanced than I was afraid she'd be. Sometimes wolves that have been without a pack get a little…"

"Crazy?" Rafe said.

"Unstable," Jace said. "But she seems to have lone wolf tendencies. Loners don't suffer from not being in a pack. But…" Rafe waited. Jace said, "Sometimes they don't have the temperament to be in one, either. They feel…hemmed in."

Rafe felt fear clutch his heart. "And you think Terin is one of those. Who's born to be a lone wolf?"

Jace sighed. "I don't know. If you're both feeling the mating bond, then she's not a true lone wolf. I'd be willing to have her in the pack, if she wanted it."

Rafe started to feel relieved, until he saw the look in Jace's eyes. "But she doesn't want it," Rafe said. "She told you that, didn't she."

Jace said, "She said that, yes. That doesn't mean she might not change her mind. Or that you couldn't still mate with her, if she were willing. But it would mean you couldn't live together full time."

Rafe had been afraid of that. It wasn't what he wanted. It would mean no cubs, for one thing, because he wouldn't want his cubs raised outside the pack, and even if he did, they were the pack's responsibility and Jace would likely insist on having them at Silverlake. He could never take cubs away from their mother.

"I don't know," he said. "I just know she's my mate. And I know she feels the bond. She just…"

"People resist the bond," Jace said. "Not often, but it happens. I think you need to at least consider the possibility that she might not want it."

Rafe shook his head. "Maybe I'll have to accept that one day," he said. "But not today, bro. Not today."

Jace bumped his shoulder. "Don't give up," he said. "Just because Emma and I fell in love in a couple of days doesn't mean that if it doesn't happen right away, it won't happen at all."

Rafe nodded. He still felt inadequate, though. If he were better, stronger, more—something—if something wasn't lacking in him, then Terin would want to bond with him. Wouldn't she?

Rafe said, "What about the hunters? Has Kane found out anything about them?"

Jace shook his head. "Not so far. He's still tracking them down. And so far his background check hasn't come up with anything on Terin. Her people may have been off the human grid. He's going to check with the Council next, to see if there is any record of her going missing."

Rafe didn't know how she'd feel about that, but if

they were after her, it had to be done. He said, "There's something you should know." He told Jace an abbreviated version of Terin's story, about her husband and the man he'd brought out to "cure" Terin.

Jace frowned. "That can't be good," he said. "If there are people trafficking in shifters…"

They might be after a "rare and exotic specimen." That thought made Rafe's blood run cold. "Or it might have something to do with her past—the part she doesn't remember, I mean."

"Maybe," Jace said. "But —"

Whatever he was going to say was cut off by the sound of a truck coming up the road. Rafe and Jace looked at each other.

"Is Terin expecting anyone?" Jace asked.

"Terin's never expecting anyone," Rafe said "No one ever comes up here."

Before they could go back into the cabin, an army truck came around the bend in the road at high speed, and slid to a stop in front of the house. Men poured out—the same ones Rafe had encountered at the cave. Their hunting dogs milled around at their feet, and they all turned to focus on Rafe and Jace.

"Damn," Jace murmured. "My gun's in the truck."

And Rafe's was in the house. "Shit," he said. "Some protectors we are."

Together they turned to face the men, who were bristling with weapons.

"We meet again," Rafe said. "How delightful. This is my friend Jace. I know I ask you this a lot, but what the fuck are you assholes doing here?"

"We're not interested in meeting your friends, dog," the leader said. "We know what you are now. And we know what that dog next to you is. Shifter filth."

"Maybe," Jace said, his voice pleasant, but with steel underneath. "But at least I'm the alpha dog." He stood on the porch without moving, arms crossed over his chest, but Rafe could feel alpha power radiating out of him. It filled him with warmth and purpose, but it had a different effect on the men—and their dogs. The dogs all started whimpering, their tails between their legs, and they lowered their bellies to the ground in submissive posture. The men tried to get them up, but they refused, whining in fear.

Rafe noticed that a couple of the men looked like they wanted to follow suit. The leader seemed unaffected. Rafe was impressed. For a human, he was pretty damn alpha.

The man shrugged. "Big deal, so you can talk to other dogs. We want the white wolf, and we've still got our guns."

Rafe heard the screen door creak, and then Emma's voice said, "Yeah. Us too."

She walked out of the house, rifle at her shoulder.

"Just one," the man sneered.

Emma kept walking, moving far enough forward so that Rafe and Jace could see two handguns stuck in the back of her jeans. Rafe's respect for Emma went up a notch.

"Actually, a couple more than that," she said.

From the window by the front door came a rifle blast. The bullet whined past the leader's head. He ducked, cursing, and while his men were distracted, Emma pulled Rafe's pistol out of the back of her jeans and tossed it to him. He caught it and cocked it, while Jace grabbed the other one. By the time the men had recovered, there were four guns trained on them.

"That was a warning shot," Rafe said. "But I gotta say, the woman behind that window is kind of a hermit, and having this many people on her land makes her a little jumpy. So, you know, one wrong move, and—pow."

Emma was scrutinizing the men. Finally she said to the leader, "Beckenham, isn't it? I thought I recognized you." She shook her head. "Still working for Alexander Grant? Or are you swimming in some other slime-filled pond now?"

He spit on the ground. "It just so happens this is professional *and* personal," he said. "I've been tracking this wolf a long time. She's a killer. Should have figured you'd be protecting her, along with the other animals."

He looked from Jace to Rafe and back again. "So which one of these is the dog you married?" he asked. He shook his head. "I can't believe that a woman who used to be civilized would mate with a zoo specimen."

Jace started growling, but the barrel of Emma's rifle never wavered. "I think it's up for debate who the animals are here," she said. She paused. "Oh, wait, it's not. So why don't you all crawl away on your bellies like the vermin you really are, and get the hell off this land?"

"Fuck you," he said. "You think I'd let a dog-whore like you order me around—"

Emma pulled the trigger. The bullet hit Beckenham in the chest, knocking him to the ground.

Shit, Rafe thought. We're dead.

But Beckenham was still breathing. He wheezed, cursing, but Rafe didn't see any blood. Either the man had on body armor, or he was a fucking vampire. The other men shifted uneasily, but they didn't shoot.

Rafe said, "You heard the lady. I'd go, if I were you. We can take a lot more damage than you can."

One of the man helped the leader up. "You bitch!" Beckenham ground out. "You wait, we'll come back and burn this mountain to the ground."

The men backed off toward their truck, keeping their guns trained on the house. They piled in, the dogs gratefully following, and peeled out.

"I guess he was wearing Kevlar," said Jace.

"I knew that," said Emma. "Really, I did."

"You could at least try to sound like you meant that," Rafe told her.

Emma shrugged. "What can I say? He pissed me off."

Jace was muttering something about "Danger Girl." Rafe shook his head. He should hang out with Emma more—it was possible she was even crazier than he was.

After making sure the men were really gone, they all trooped back into the cabin.

Terin was in the corner, shaking. Rafe went over to put his arms around her, but she wrapped her arms around herself, keeping him away. "That man," she said.

"Do you know him?" Jace asked.

Terin shook her head, not looking at anyone.

"Terin?" Rafe asked gently. "It's okay. They're gone." He started rubbing the outsides of her arms gently, as if he were trying to warm her. But he could see the cold was inside her. "You're fine," he said softly. "You did great."

"I agree," Jace said. He was frowning at Terin. He needed to stop that. Couldn't he see she was upset?

Jace added, "But those men aren't going to give up."

"Not if they're working for Alexander Grant," Emma added.

Tern frowned. She'd stopped shaking and her eyes were more focused. "Who's Alexander Grant?" she asked.

"Emma's ex," Rafe said. "A very, very bad man, who hates us a lot."

"What does he want with me?" Terin asked.

"I don't know," Jace said.

Emma asked, "Terin, did you know that man?"

Terin's eye grew unfocused again. "No," she said. "I don't know. I don't remember ever seeing him before, but I felt like I knew him."

They all looked at each other. "Someone from your past?" Rafe asked.

"I don't *know!*" She pushed his hands away.

Rafe looked at Jace helplessly. "She can't stay here now."

"You can't make me go," Terin said.

"He's right, Terin," Emma said quietly. "Those men will be back, and probably with more firepower. I know you don't want to leave here, but I think Rafe is right. The only place you'll be safe right now is at Silverlake."

Terin looked at them all gathered around her, her eyes getting wild. Rafe could feel the panic building in her.

He reached out to comfort her once more, but she batted his hands away. "No!" she said. "This is your fault, all of you! Nobody bothered me until you came here. Nobody even knew I was here! And now you crowd around me and want to take me away and make me go somewhere where there are people...people all the time...and I can't get away. I can't breathe! I can't take this. The people, everybody telling me what to do. Why can't you all just leave me alone?"

"Terin," Rafe began, but she wouldn't listen. She shifted, flowing out of her dress, and jumped through the window out into the yard. In moments, she'd disappeared into the woods.

CHAPTER 16

Terin ran and ran, until she was exhausted. As if she could outrun the trouble, and the danger, and all the things she couldn't remember.

Even more, she wanted to outrun all the expectations people had of her, all her feelings, all the love that Rafe had for her that she was so frightened of.

It was all so *much*. Too much for her. She was used to quiet and solitude. And now there were armed men invading her property, and all these people were there, wanting to help, wanting her to do things and react and care about them and like them.

She just couldn't.

Finally she reached the mountaintop and lay spent, letting the wind ruffle her fur, until she could feel like a part of the land and the wind and the trees and the sky. She felt as if it were all passing through her, her body dissolving so she could float among the stars like the spirit wolf that some people called her.

What did those men want? Why were they hunting her? Why *now*? Had she always been a monster? Had she done even more bad things than she could remember?

She couldn't stop thinking about Rafe. She wished desperately that she could just wrap herself in his arms and shut out the whole rest of the world. She wanted that unspoken understanding that she'd felt when they were making love, or when they were just sitting outside on the porch swing, baring their souls to each other.

She didn't want him to endanger himself for her. She didn't want him to *want* so much from her. Why couldn't he just let things be easy between them?

But she had no answer to that. She didn't think she ever would.

The sun went down and the stars came out. Terin watched them wheel majestically through the sky. She was scared. Scared of the men, and scared of losing Rafe. She felt empty without him. Much more than she had felt when Ben died. She had missed Ben, but she'd also enjoyed the freedom to finally be herself, without hiding her wolf from him.

But when it was just her and Rafe, she felt like maybe she could be herself. He didn't seem to mind all the things that were strange about her. He was a shifter too, so she didn't have to hide that from him. And he cared about her. He wanted her to be happy.

He wanted to love her. And she loved him. She just didn't want to let him down, and she didn't want to be disappointed.

Now that her panic had receded, she was wondering if there was some way she could try being with the pack. At least go to Silverlake, and see what it was like. The idea of leaving her cabin, her home, scared her. It was the only place she belonged, the only place she could remember.

But what if those men came back? And what if they hurt Rafe, because she wouldn't go to Silverlake and be safe there?

It was late when she got to her feet and loped slowly down the mountain, making her way soft-footed through the woods. It was a moonlit night, and she stayed in the shadows so the light wouldn't glint off her fur.

As she neared the cabin, she became aware of a strong scent. Burning wood. Thick, oily smoke. Not like a woodstove—more like someone burning trash. Only stronger. So strong…

Fire.

She sped up, dashing through the woods, not wanting to believe what she knew she was going to see. She burst out of the woods at the edge of the clearing and skidded to a stop, gazing in horror.

Her cabin was destroyed. Those men had come back while she was up the mountain, and burned her home. Flames still licked the half-collapsed walls. Her books, her paintings, her quilt, her dishes and decorations. Her herbs. All the things that meant so much to her, that made her feel secure. Everything was gone.

She stood staring, unable to take it in. Rafe's and Jace's trucks were gone—they must have left just after she did. After she'd rejected their offers of help, after she'd run away from Jace and Emma's kindness and

Rafe's love.

And she'd been punished. The hunters had come back, and when they hadn't been able to find her, they'd burned her home down in retaliation.

And maybe as a warning.

Now she had nowhere to go. Nothing she could do. Rafe wouldn't want her now, and Jace and Emma wouldn't take her in.

She was alone and homeless, just like she'd been ten years ago.

Broken.

A howl welled up in her chest, into her throat, and she put her head up and cried to the sky. All the hurt and pain, all the loneliness, all the anger at the unfairness of it. This time she'd hurt no one. She'd only attacked to defend herself. She'd never meant harm to anyone, and people just kept getting hurt because of her.

She howled again, backing into the woods, wanting to hide herself from the sight of her ruined home. She was so distraught that she wasn't paying attention to anything around her, her nose filled with acrid smoke. So she didn't sense him until he grabbed her.

A man launched himself out of the trees and hit her in a flying tackle, imprisoning her in his arms. His momentum brought them to the ground, rolling over, and she squirmed frantically, snapping at him. He wrapped one hand around her muzzle so she couldn't bite, and whispered in her ear.

"Shhh. It's okay. It's me, Rafe."

Rafe? What was he doing here? Terin went limp,

stunned. He held her close, still holding her muzzle closed while he murmured in her ear, his breath ruffling her fur.

"You have to be quiet, okay?" he said. "Those guys are still out there, waiting for you. They must have figured if they burned the cabin, you wouldn't be able to scent them in all the smoke."

Or they'd just done it to be vindictive.

She dipped her head in acknowledgement of his warning. He kissed her between the ears and then loosened his grip on her.

She changed back into human form and fell into his arms, tears rolling down her face. "My cabin," she said, burying the words in his chest. "All my things, Rafe. Everything's gone."

He stroked her back, her hair. "It's okay," he murmured in her ear. "It's okay. Don't worry about that now." But it wasn't okay. He had his pack, his home. She had nothing.

"What are you doing here?" she whispered, pulling herself together. "Where's your truck?"

"I didn't want them to know I was here," he said. "No time to explain now. They're coming." He pulled back and put his hands on either side of her face, looking deeply into her eyes. She could see his eyes glittering gold in the darkness. He said, "I'm going to get you out of here, and we're going to get these guys for good. But I need you to follow my lead, and you have to trust me completely and do what I say, no matter how crazy it seems. Can you do that?"

She stared into his eyes, hands on his chest. Her own words came back to her: *I don't trust anyone.* She never had—not even Ben, even when he was being kind to her. She'd always held part of herself back.

But Rafe had come for her. He'd made a plan to keep her safe. He was risking his life for her.

She nodded. "Okay," she said.

His face lit up with his cocky, reckless smile. "Okay, babe," he said. "I need you to shift, and follow my cues. Whatever I tell you to do, promise—*promise* you'll do it."

"I promise," she said.

He gave her a quick kiss. "Okay, then. Let's do this, ghost wolf." And they both shifted into their wolf shapes.

Rafe moved slowly at first, slinking through the woods like a shadow, sniffing the air as if casting about for a scent. Terin couldn't understand why he didn't just run, leading her back to Silverlake, to the pack territory where they'd be safe.

But she'd promised to trust him.

Suddenly, Rafe's head went up, and he turned his head he caught a scent. A moment later, she scented it too. The men. Their dogs. And the sharp metallic smell of their guns.

Rafe led her closer to the men—closer, closer. Surely he wasn't going to attack them? He stopped and nosed Terin briefly, and then stepped out of the woods into the moonlight.

A man called out softly, "There!" and she heard the

crackle of radios. "We've got the black one." Then, more faintly, "Hold your fire. Track it—it might lead you to the white one—or to its pack." Rafe took a cautious step, then looked back at her.

He wanted her to step out there? Expose herself? He had to be insane.

But she could see her promise in his eyes. *Trust me.*

Gathering all her courage, Terin stepped out of the forest. The moonlight caught her white fur, and the dying flames of the cabin turned one side of her a dull red. She heard a shout, and the radios went crazy.

"There she is!"

"We've got them both."

"In pursuit."

And then there was a cacophony of barking. They'd brought out the dogs.

Rafe turned and ran, cutting straight across the clearing. Terin followed, plunging into the woods after him. She could hear the men and dogs behind them. The sound made her want to run flat out, as fast as she could, but Rafe was keeping a moderate pace. Was he afraid of outpacing her? Or did he have some other reason? She increased her speed, coming level with him and pulling ahead. His response was to slow down.

So he didn't want to go too fast—he didn't want to lose their pursuers. This must be part of the plan, but Terin hoped to hell he knew what he was doing. The fur was standing up all down her back, anticipating the feel of a bullet.

A tranquilizer dart buzzed through the woods and

thunked into a tree near her. After that, a bullet whined by Rafe. So they wanted her alive, but they didn't care if they killed Rafe. That made her furious. And scared.

Rafe increased the pace, increasing their lead—but not too much. She could see now that he was trying to keep them out of range of the men's guns without losing them completely. The men fell back, and Terin thought they would be okay.

Until they loosed the dogs.

The dogs could go faster than the humans, and they could follow the shifters' scent. Terin knew enough about hunting to know that the dogs were trained to follow them, surround them, trap them until the hunters came.

The dogs bayed, and Terin's heart came into her throat. She was just about to forget her promise, forget everything and run for her life, when she became aware of other wolves around her in the forest. They were shadowing her and Rafe, running parallel to them, just out of sight. Silent and deadly.

Rafe's pack.

Trust me.

The dogs ran faster, barking and belling, not far behind them now. Rafe swerved suddenly, skirting a grove of trees, and Terin scrambled to follow him. The brush was getting thicker now, and the dogs followed their trail in a wide curve, spreading out.

A thick, curved wall of brush loomed up in front of them—a dead end. Terin went to go around it, and then realized that Rafe was heading straight in.

This was exactly what the dogs had been trained for. They'd be trapped, torn to pieces by the dogs or caught by the hunters. Terin gave a warning bark, but Rafe just glanced back over his shoulder at her and kept going.

You have to do what I say, no matter how crazy it seems. Promise me.

She hesitated for a split second, and then she plunged after Rafe, straight into the trap.

The dogs followed, penning them in. Rafe turned on them, snarling a warning, and Terin joined him. But the dogs were well-trained to trap their prey—to wait for an order from their master before tearing it apart.

Terin waited, heart pounding. Where was the rest of the pack? Why had they left her and Rafe to fend for themselves? She heard the hunters crashing through the forest, and finally they appeared, following the dogs. The leader—Beckenham—raised his rifle and aimed it at Rafe.

"You should have let me take the white wolf earlier today," he said. "At least I would have let you live. But Grant's woman gave me a cracked rib and I'm pissed off, so your girlfriend gets to watch you die, and then I'm going to finish what that little white bitch started all those years ago."

All those years ago? What was he talking about?

Rafe growled. Terin gathered herself for a desperate leap at Beckenham. She couldn't let him hurt Rafe. Everything seemed to be moving in slow motion—the gun barrels being raised, the evil smile on Beckenham's face, her own body. She was just about to launch herself when she heard a sharp command from behind her. "Now!"

There was a rush of snapping sounds, and suddenly four of Beckenham's men were upside down, dangling by their ankles from the trees. One was knocked to the ground by a gray and brown wolf. Beckenham whirled, trying to bring up his rifle to shoot the wolf, but there was an immediate symphony of ammo sliding into chambers, and half a dozen men and women stepped out of the forest, guns trained on him. And every one of them had a wolf by their side.

CHAPTER 17

Jace stepped out of the cover of the trees, and Terin felt a wave of alpha dominance roll over her. The dogs immediately rolled over and showed their bellies, or slunk away with their tails between their legs. It was all Terin could do not to join them. Then, behind Jace, Terin saw a huge grizzly bear step out of the woods as well, and rear up on his hind legs, giving a great roar before it dropped down onto all fours again.

Holy shit.

"Drop your weapons," Jace said. "That includes you up in the trees. And no tricks. Emma's kind of pissed about the Kevlar thing, and this time she's going to be aiming for heads."

The men hanging from the rope traps dropped their weapons to the ground, and a huge man with a face like granite came up and searched the man on the ground, taking away all his weapons as well.

Beckenham had dropped the barrel of his rifle, but when the stone-faced man stepped toward him, he brought it up again. "I'll keep mine, thanks," he said.

Jace raised a brief hand to the stone-faced man, and he stopped where he was, but he kept Beckenham covered with his own weapon.

"Look, we've got nothing against you personally," Beckenham said, trying to sound conciliatory. If Terin was in human form, she would have snorted. Like he hadn't called her and Rafe 'dogs' and burned down her cabin out of revenge for being humiliated. He went on, "You don't know what you're harboring here. The white one has bad blood. I'm doing you a favor—"

Rafe growled again.

"A favor?" Jace said. "Is that what you call arson, assault, attempted murder and kidnapping?"

The man snorted with derision. All the wolves and most of the people growled simultaneously, and most of the wolves started moving forward.

The man said, "You're not going to kill us. Your boy Kane, there," he nodded at the stone-faced man, "has been in town inquiring about us. If we disappear, it's going to come right back on you. And you've brought enough trouble on yourselves from Grant without adding to it. So I'll give you one more chance to do this the easy way. Just give us the white wolf, and we'll leave the rest of you alone."

"I don't think so," said Jace. "But I would like to know what you want her for. And how you and Alexander Grant even knew she was here."

Beckenham said, "What the hell do you care? She's not even in your pack."

Emma called out, "Oh, for God's sake. Can I just shoot him already?"

"Not yet, sweetheart," Jace called back. "And I'm

thinking Rafe has first dibs." Rafe bared his teeth. Beckenham stared him down.

Terin was still trembling. There was something horribly familiar about this man, even though she didn't know him. It was like the feeling she'd had when she first woke up at Ben's—that she was in danger, but she didn't know why or from who.

Now she knew. This man knew who she was. He knew what she'd done before. He knew all the things she didn't know.

All the things she'd never wanted to know.

Jace returned his attention to Beckenham. "Aside from the fact that I don't believe in turning innocent people over to murderers and kidnappers, the white wolf happens to be under the protection of the Silverlake pack. You're not leaving here with her."

"Fine," the man said. "My plans are flexible." He looked as if he was going to lower his weapon, but at the last moment he swung the rifle barrel up and shot straight at Terin.

Before Terin could move, Rafe barreled into her side, pushing her out of the path of the bullet. It whined past, missing them both by inches. Then Rafe gathered his feet under him and launched himself straight at Beckenham.

It was all over in seconds. The man lay on the ground, throat torn out.

The other man on the ground raised his hands. "Hey, man, this is just a job for us. Just because Frank had a thing about the white one doesn't mean we want to give our lives for this. Call it quits, and we're outta here."

Jace and Kane exchanged looks, and then Jace made a gesture of dismissal. Terin was relieved. She didn't want any more killing.

Emma stepped forward. "You give Alexander Grant a message from Emma Wilkes," she said. "Tell him to stay the hell out of our mountains. If we ever see—or even smell—any of you here again, you're going to end up like your friend Frank. And that goes for Grant, too."

"When you put it that way," Jace said thoughtfully, "why don't you tell Grant he can come on by? We'll be waiting."

Rafe bared his teeth and growled.

"The rest of you," Jace said, "no second chances."

He turned to Kane. "Get rid of them," he said.

CHAPTER 18

It turned out that the pack had trucks hidden on a nearby logging road. Those in human form piled into them, taking the men's weapons with them. The others, still in wolf form, moved off through the woods, making their own way back to Silverlake.

Rafe shifted to human form, and Terin followed his lead. Somebody handed her some clothes out of the back of one of the trucks, and she put them on mechanically, too exhausted and shell-shocked to really know what she was doing.

Rafe boosted her up into the back of one of the pickups and sat down next to her in the truck bed, holding her protectively. She was trembling with reaction.

"He knew me," Terin said numbly. "He knew who I am. Where I come from."

And now he was dead, and they might never find out what he knew. She didn't know if she was glad or sorry about that.

"It's okay," Rafe murmured, stroking her hair. "It doesn't matter." She could feel love and reassurance radiating out of him, and gradually she calmed down.

They rode back to the Silverlake compound, the two of them holding each other in silence. The others were talking and joking, high on the adrenalin and the victory. By the time they arrived, the rest of the wolves were drifting in from the woods, shifting and getting dressed.

Rafe lifted Terin down from the back of the truck, and she looked around at all the people. "They fought for me," she whispered to Rafe, overwhelmed. "Why did they do that?"

Rafe smiled. "Because I asked them to," he said simply. "Because we're pack. And now you're pack, too." His smile faded a little. "At least, I hope you'll want to be."

A gruff older man said, "God, I hope so too. Anybody who can get this jerk to act like an adult for five minutes is somebody we need around here."

"Shut up, Mick," Rafe growled.

Mick winked at Terin.

Terin leaned on Rafe. "When did you act like an adult?" she asked innocently. "I must have missed that part."

Mick laughed. "I like her," he said.

Rafe growled again, but he crooked his arm around her neck and kissed the top of her head.

Other pack members came up, one by one, and spoke to Rafe. They all wanted to touch him—a one-armed hug, a slap on the back, a touch on the arm. Most of them touched her, too, more gently.

"I hope you don't mind the touching," Rafe

whispered. "It's kind of a pack thing."

Terin shook her head. She'd expected it to feel overwhelming, but Rafe was right—it was comforting. It made her feel like maybe she could belong.

Finally the group started to disperse. "Come on," Rafe said. "You've had a hell of a day—you need some rest. Let's get you settled in."

That brought everything crashing back down around Terin. She was going to be sleeping in a borrowed place with nothing of her own. It was all gone.

She looked around. There were cabins dotting the area, light pouring out their windows, looking warm and welcoming. But Rafe was taking her along a dirt path that wound up the darkened hillside. "Where are we going?" she asked.

He just said, "You'll see. But it's not the bachelor crack den of horror. That would be too cruel, after the day you've had."

She tried to smile, but she was so tired she could barely put one foot in front of the other. She stumbled over a rock, and Rafe scooped her up in his arms, cradling her gently.

"What are you doing?" Terin asked. Her arms automatically twined around his neck.

"Taking care of my future mate," Rafe said.

"I'm too heavy," she protested, but at the same time she snuggled closer to him.

"You weigh practically nothing," Rafe said. "I'm going to have to start feeding you up."

"Uh huh," Terin said. "Says the Destroyer of

Carrots. Who exactly is going to be cooking all this fattening food, again?"

"Hmm," he said. "I'll get back to you on that."

"Yeah," she said. "Me, that's who." He laughed.

She started thinking about her kitchen, about making him food, and realized once more that it was all gone. Her favorite platter, all her dishes and books and paintings—the loss hit her again, and a tear trickled down her face.

"Hey, shh, it's okay," Rafe said softly, kissing it away. "We're almost there."

They crested the hill and came to a cabin set off from the rest. It also had welcoming lights shining in its windows. Rafe put her down at the front steps.

"If this isn't your crack den, then whose is it?" Terin asked.

"Mick's," Rafe said. "He's kind of a curmudgeon, so he build his cabin up here away from the rabble of us young whippersnappers. We thought you might be more comfortable up here out of the crowds, so he swapped with me. I totally owe him for that, by the way, and a couple of blueberry pies would go a long way toward canceling my debt. Just sayin'."

Terin couldn't answer. She was exhausted and overwhelmed, and she just wanted to sink down somewhere and mourn over what she'd lost. Then maybe she could appreciate what they'd done for her.

They opened the cabin door and walked inside. Terin took one look around and caught her breath, stunned.

All her things were here. Her paintings were stacked against the wall, and her paints and brushes and other art supplies were boxed up nearby. The bed had her quilt spread over it, and her dishes were stacked in the kitchen—even her favorite platter. Her clothes had been hung up in the makeshift closet. And her books lined one entire wall—boxes and bags of books.

Terin's knees gave way and she sank down on the couch, tears pouring down her face. "I don't understand," she said. "How did this happen?"

Rafe sat down next to her. "After you left this afternoon, we were afraid that Beckenham would make good on his threat to burn you out. Jace and I talked it over, and then he and Emma and I packed up everything we could and got it out of there. We figured if we were wrong, we could always bring it back."

When she was silent, he added, "I know we did it without your permission, but I hope you're okay with it."

She turned and flung her arms around his neck. "I can't believe you all did this for me," she whispered into his chest. "It must have taken hours. And then you built the traps and set up the plan, and came back for me…"

And she'd been sitting at the top of the mountain feeling sorry for herself.

"I don't deserve you," she said to Rafe.

He laughed softly. "I'm sure a lot of the pack would agree with you," he said. "They'd say no woman deserves to have to put up with me."

She shook her head. "They'd don't know you like I

do."

He grinned. "You just keep telling yourself that."

He stood up and scooped her up off the couch. "Now I'm putting you to bed," he informed her. "You're so exhausted you can barely talk."

Terin let him carry her over to the bed, but when he put her down, she refused to let go of his neck, pulling him down beside her.

"You can't put me to bed all alone," she said. "That would be cruel."

His smile grew wider, and he lay down beside her, taking her in his arms. He began kissing her softly, gently, but soon their hunger rose up and they were devouring each other, kissing and stroking and tasting, wanting to be a part of each other.

Their clothes slid to the floor. Terin couldn't wait to feel Rafe inside her, joining the two of them, making him hers forever. But as he moved over her, she pressed her hands against his chest, stopping him. "Wait," she said. "Before we…you know…I want to invoke the mating bond."

He looked deeply into her eyes, cupping her face in his hands. She could see the longing in his eyes, but he said, "You've been through a lot tonight. This isn't the time to make life-changing decisions."

She shook her head. "It's exactly the time," she said.

She'd always held back, always been afraid to trust. She had her reasons, but she'd realized that didn't matter. Rafe had offered her everything he had, everything he was. He was all in—and that was all she could ever ask.

She stroked his wild, unruly hair back from his forehead. "I want you," she said. "No one else has ever cared for me the way you do. No one has ever done so much for me."

He shook his head and tried to say something, but she put her finger against his lips and went on.

"And no one else has ever made me want to make him feel the same. Every time I look at you, I just want to heal all the hurts inside you. To love you and treasure you and make you understand how special you are, what a good man you are. How you deserve to be the center of someone's world. The favorite. The best."

Rafe's eyes filled with tears. Slowly, he bent his head and kissed her.

"You're my favorite, Rafe Connors," she whispered. "My mate. I want you above everyone else, always, and I'll do everything I can to make you happy."

Twining his fingers with hers, he moved slowly, pressing into her, filling her up. She gave herself completely to him, and she felt the magic roaring through them, swirling around them, making them one, exploding into stars and bathing them in the colors of the northern lights.

EPILOGUE

Rafe bounded into the bedroom of the new cabin he shared with Terin, picked her up, and twirled her around before giving her a smacking kiss and setting her on the ground again.

"Hi," he said.

She gave him her tiny smile. "Hi, yourself," she said. "What was that enthusiastic greeting for?"

"I missed you," he said. "I've been gone a really long time."

"Four hours is a long time," she agreed, her face grave but her eyes twinkling. "During that eternity, I decided we should put the bed on this wall, under the skylight, so we can look up at the stars."

He nodded. "I like it," he said. "I concur. Guess what I brought you from town?"

Her face lit up in the way he loved.

"A present?" she said. She came over and started sticking her hands in his pockets. "Where where where?"

"Greedy," he said, grabbing for her hands. He conveniently missed the one that was moving down the front of his pants.

Terin wrapped her hand around his cock. "Is this the present?"

Rafe totally lost his focus. "Uhh, what?" He gathered his thoughts together with difficulty. "No. I mean yes, you can have that whenever you want. But I actually brought you some of those chocolate caramels you like." He fished the bag out of his jacket pocket.

"Mmm, yummy," she said, letting go of his cock and taking the bag. She slid her arms around his neck. "You know you're my favorite, right?"

"Your favorite mate?" he teased.

"My favorite everything. Lover, mate, friend, protector, candy enabler."

He wrapped his arms around her. "No offense, but you don't have a lot of basis for comparison."

She kissed him lightly. "Lucky for you, then, I guess."

He grinned at her, his heart expanding in his chest. "Yup. Lucky for me. You know I can never let you down off this mountain, because you'll immediately find some guy better than me."

She kissed him again. "I like you. And besides, I'm pregnant. What other guy would put up with your progeny? He's probably going to be a holy terror."

He stood there like an idiot, his mouth hanging open. After a couple of tries, he managed to gasp out, "You're pregnant?"

He swept her up into his arms, swinging her around again. "You're pregnant." Oh, shit. Should he be doing that? He put her down. "Wait. Was I squishing you too hard? Are you okay with this? Are you happy?"

She started giggling. "Um. You know that hugging me won't squish the baby out like toothpaste out of a tube, right?"

He kissed her nose. "It might. Why take chances?"

She locked her arms around his waist. "And yes, I'm happy. Happier than I ever thought I could be."

He could feel that she was telling the truth. Her happiness radiated out of her and warmed his own heart. He breathed a sigh of relief. "Good. Me too. But I guess you figured that out."

"Uh huh," she said. "I made you a present, too."

She let him go and went over to the corner, where a painting was propped with its face to the wall.

Terin picked it up and turned it around. Rafe caught his breath. A black wolf and a white wolf sat on the top of a mountain under a star-spangled sky, their muzzles raised to the full moon above. A rainbow of lights surrounded them, illuminating a valley full of wolves below. And at their feet, barely visible, was a black wolf cub.

Rafe slid his arms around her, cradling her close. "Best present ever," he said.

Come to Silverlake Mountain and fall in love...

Smokin' hot shifter men with hearts of gold; the strong, passionate women who love them; secrets, lies and danger; naughty, steamy love scenes—and happily ever afters.

NEXT UP:

Tiger Mate (Jesse's story)

Silverlake Enforcers
The Enforcers: KANE
The Enforcers: ISRAEL
The Enforcers: NOAH

ABOUT THE AUTHOR

Anastasia Wilde lives in the deep forests of the Pacific Northwest, where sexy shifters may or may not be found hiding among the tall, ancient trees. She writes hot paranormal romances about wild, passionate shifter men and the strong women who are destined to win their hearts. Broken, complicated, devoted, protective—love heals their wounds and smooths their rough edges (but not too much!). When not writing, Anastasia is traveling, nomming on any food involving bacon or melty cheese (ideally both), adding to her magical crystal collection, or relaxing with a glass of wine, watching the sun set behind the mountains.

Follow Anastasia on Facebook:
https://www.facebook.com/anastasiawildeauthor/

Made in United States
North Haven, CT
17 April 2022